POUR DECISIONS

A KATIE MURPHY COZY MYSTERY

SUZANNE BOLDEN

LAUGHING DEER PRESS

CONTENTS

CHAPTER ONE

I took a moment to inhale the humid evening air before slowly releasing it from my lungs. After shutting the car off, I allowed my eyelids to close for just a moment. I'd landed safely back at the cottage. Between the Wisconsin snow I left behind and the chilly temperatures on my drive south, I didn't warm up until I crossed over the Florida state line and drove to Seaside Cove.

The sun dipping below the horizon created a tranquil atmosphere on the quaint side street and bathed the cottage in a soft light. I unlatched the gate of the white picket fence and walked up the steppingstones that led to the small porch of Kenmare Cottage. The border of the fence was edged with miniature roses and jasmine bushes. Their blooms filled the air with a delicate fragrance that relaxed me. Climbing vines splashed with red, orange, yellow, and purple flowers cascaded over the porch railing while pots overflowing with geraniums greeted me at the front door.

I caught a glimpse of my aunt, Maeve Murphy, inside. Her hands gently massaged Paddy's shoulders while he sat in his recliner. He looked worn out. Poor guy. His lifelong dream project of opening an Irish Pub has been a stressful process.

I tapped lightly before pushing the door open.

Maeve greeted me with open arms. "Katie girl, you made it home safely!" Her hugs were like a cozy blanket, making me feel warm and loved.

"I didn't want to disturb you guys, because you looked so cute giving Paddy that shoulder rub."

"Ah sure lass, his knots be multiplying by the day." Maeve stepped aside as I entered. "But come on in now. You must be famished. I've got some leftovers I can heat up."

"No need. I grabbed a gas station sandwich last time I filled up."

"Give your Uncle Paddy a good squeeze first, lassie." Paddy stood and I wrapped my arms around him. 'How is everyone back in Wisconsin? I miss me family and mates there."

"Dermot and Grace are well and send greetings for a

happy New Year. Oh, and good news for our family. They are welcoming a daughter-in-law!"

"So young Patrick is to be wed? What a blessing for them," Maeve said.

I was relieved that she didn't bring up the fact I wasn't married yet, even though I was older than my cousin. "Ginger's such a sweetie. She owns the bookstore in Harmony. Mom and Dad video-chatted with us all from Ireland. They were happy to see me with family this year since I didn't make it home to them. The village held a Winter Wonderland festival, and packed away in my luggage is a little gift for you. But for now, will you be having the grand opening before I have to leave?"

The reason behind my decision to take a break from my business in Los Angeles was still fresh in my mind. Staying away from Joel, my ex-boyfriend, seemed like the best course of action at the moment, and stalling my departure until after the pub's opening was a wonderful excuse.

"We hope so. When are you leaving us?" Maeve asked.

"I called my assistant Kristen from the road, and I can stay here another week without a problem. She assured me all the holiday parties had gone off without a hitch except for some New Year's Eve shenanigans at one in Beverly Hills. Thankfully, she managed to keep it out of the tabloids. She's a numero uno asset to KM Party Planners."

Apparently, the ongoing saga continued when Paddy explained that things were still moving slowly regarding permitting and inspections. "Mayor Trimble promised certain things would move along after the holidays when people were back to work, but I'm not holding my breath."

Uncle Paddy was not known for cussing, at least not out loud and while ladies were present, but when I'd first arrived here in Florida last December, I overheard a phone conversation where I got an earful. It sounded like this Mayor Trimble was causing grief for my sweet Irish uncle. I wasn't privy to the details, but I've met people who, given a little bit of power, go all in on it, leaving bodies in their wake.

"They won't keep me down by gosh. This old coot is not going to fade away quietly," Paddy added.

"You are an old coot for sure." Maeve chuckled. "But I love you and will be by your side, no matter how crazy you get."

Irish families are renowned for their warmth and hospitality, and Uncle Paddy and Aunt Maeve were no exception. When they invited me to visit their new home on the Florida Panhandle, I eagerly accepted, knowing that I would be treated like a daughter. Officially, we may be cousins or something similar, but we don't bother with titles. They are simply my beloved aunt and uncle.

"I'll bet you are ready for sleep," Maeve said. "Bed is turned down for you."

"Even though I've been dreaming about slipping between those cool, smooth, cedar-scented sheets and pulling that quilt up under my chin again, I believe I'll take a walk first. I've been sitting in my car way too much the past couple of days."

CHAPTER TWO

My evening walk took me down Heron Street toward the riverfront. I turned onto Main Street to admire the remnants of the holiday season that still adorned the quaint shops that lined the street.

The Sew-Sew Shop featured Christmas quilted wall hangings. This is where Maeve's sewing circle met and where she'd created the quilt that I was lucky enough to be sleeping under tonight. Maeve had always built a community of friends around herself because she embodied the cheerful Irish demeanor known around the world.

The window display in the bookstore had already moved on from the Christmas season and showcased books by local authors. A small sign reminded passersby to support their community by shopping locally and using any gift certificates they may have received. One author, a local fisherman, wrote about life on the Wimico River. There was a small guide to identifying seashells on the Gulf of Mexico by a resident who proudly listed her accreditations. I began to continue on my way when one of the other books caught my eye. It was an E.L. Brooks crime thriller! Wow! It seemed like fate that I'd bought one from Ginger's Book Nook in Harmony and had planned to read it on the beach here. How cool is that?

The local tourist souvenir shop was really a step up from those usually seen in coastal areas. It had the typical T-shirts and seashells but also stunning artistic creations using sea glass and pieces of driftwood. I reminded myself to grab one of their baseball caps with the city's name on it before I left. Hmm…did Paddy have any wearables for customers to purchase? Tourists loved that sort of thing. A T-shirt with the logo of an Irish Pub was sure to be a good marketing idea.

On the opposite side of Main Street stood Paddy's Pub, its front facade grand and balanced. The two stories were adorned with large windows that looked out onto Main Street, a reminder of its past life as a bank when small towns took pride in local institutions and their buildings reflected their success. Nowadays, big banking institutions dominated with branches all over and sleek modern buildings, while customers preferred online transactions.

Lights were on inside, so it appeared that construction crews were working overtime to get everything done. I couldn't help but hope that Paddy would have the chance to open before I left town.

I continued on Main until the commercial area transitioned into a residential neighborhood. The land gently sloped downward, leading to Wimico Bay. Here, grand homes lined the streets, enjoying picturesque views of the bay, Horseshoe Island, and the endless waters of the Gulf of Mexico. I made my way down to the paved path that would take me back toward the river, past the wharves and marina area.

The setting sun painted a gentle orange and pink hue across the sky, reflecting off the calm waters of the bay. Palm trees swayed in the breeze, their fronds gently rustling. The crisp, salty air wafted in from the Gulf, mixing with the smell of flowers and freshly mown grass. A distant boat horn echoed along the shoreline.

A young couple approached me, walking a small beagle and a larger golden doodle. Their voices were low and friendly as they talked to each other, and their laughter echoed brightly through the twilight. We nodded in greeting as the doodle brushed against my leg. His tail wagged furiously as I petted him while the beagle pounced playfully at my ankles.

"Bet these guys love to take this evening walk," I said, bending to rub the beagle behind his ears.

"Not as much as we do," the woman responded. "Hope they're not bothering you."

"Not at all," I answered. "Enjoy the rest of your evening."

"You as well."

What a pleasant little town, I thought. I'm feeling so relaxed here as I continued along the edge of the bay. Above me, I saw the causeway stretching across to Horseshoe Island. Then the path bent, following the edge of the river's mouth. As I neared the marina, I noted light-hearted laughter and conversation on some of the larger boats, accompanied by soft music and the clinking and clattering of sailboat masts.

Gator's Seafood Grill and Raw Oyster Bar establishment was open. I caught just a corner of the back deck facing the river, its patio lighting reflected in the dark river. The adjacent seafood market was dark now, but it would be bustling with activity in the early morning hours of darkness as the fishing boats left the harbor for open waters, returning hours later with their catch of the day.

I was still a few blocks from Heron when the area

turned grittier with a smattering of small engine repair shops, bait shops, old motels and mish-mash of abandoned buildings with rusted metal roofs.

Three motorcycles revved their engines as they passed me and turned into the parking lot of a business up ahead. Light from a side door of the building spilled out as a person hefted a garbage bag into a big trash container and went back inside the bar. Where Gator's outside deck faced the water, this Salty Dawg bar turned its back to the river where small, weathered boats were tied to dilapidated docks. Neon beer signs flashed in high, narrow, rectangular windows.

A figure exited the main door, his coarse features lit briefly by the single bulb fixture above the concrete stoop. He didn't notice me as the tip of his cigarette flared red, and he walked around the corner of the building and into the shadows, where I lost sight of him.

My phone vibrating in my pocket startled me. I stopped to check the text coming in, hoping it was Kristen letting me know the extremely fussy movie star's party had gone well. That's when I heard voices coming from the darkness.

"Come on, Junior. Don't make me put together a story that Butch don't wanna hear. He just wants what Vinnie owes him. Now."

"Back off. I'm not Vinnie's boy anymore."

"Not the way I see it."

A scuffing sound.

"Get your hands off me. I need more time."

I couldn't quite decipher the rest of the mumbling from the man around the corner, but he soon reappeared and threw his cigarette to the ground, angrily grinding it into the gravel with his boot. I didn't want to stick around to see who else might come out, so I hurriedly crossed River Road, cutting the angle to get to the streetlight on the corner of Heron.

CHAPTER THREE

I made my way back to the cottage along the dark streets and saw Paddy emerge from the front door, muttering to himself. He didn't notice me and almost collided with me. "Lordy lass, but you gave me a start!" His smile quickly disappeared as he walked past me and headed toward his golf cart.

A low voice said, "Don't know how much more the man can take." Maeve rested her hands on the porch railing, watching Paddy until he turned the corner and was out of sight. "Did you enjoy your stroll?"

There must be more trouble at the pub. "It was okay. But what happened now? Why is Paddy so upset?"

"The electricians were working late, and the one with the key left early, so they couldn't lock up. They gave Paddy a call, and he went down to lock the pub up.

All the stress that's building up inside the man..." She sighed and shook her head. "Not good for a body."

"So, did they figure out what the electrical problems were?"

Maeve explained that the food products that needed to be kept cold had been moved into a temporary refrigerated trailer along with the kegs of beer because of unexplained power outages. She speculated that they were addressing that. "Which would be grand because the freezer unit's noisy generators were starting to annoy neighboring businesses."

"I tell y'all, they better get it right. I just can't figure out for the life of me what in tarnation is so darned difficult about wiring a business that Sammy's boys can't get done."

I squinted toward the source of the voice and saw a gray-haired woman stepping into the glow of our porch light. She had a sturdy frame, with generous curves and soft, wrinkled skin that showed her age. Her eyes held a wisdom and her lips curved up in a friendly grin.

"Who's this gal, Maeve? Company from home?" she asked in her deep and husky voice. "She's got that red hair of your people if my eyes aren't deceiving me."

"Your eyes are deceiving you, Winnie. You met her before Christmas, didn't you? This is my niece Katie Murphy, and her hair is auburn, not red, as she will let you know. She lives in Los Angeles but grew up in Ireland." Maeve gave me a quick wink.

"Los Angeleeese? Good lord, who would want to live there?" Winnie pronounced. "You can keep them big cities."

"Weren't you just in Atlanta visiting your son over Christmas?"

"I tell ya, that trip just solidified my notion 'bout them big ol' cities. If it weren't for him being there, I wouldn't set foot in the place. But next year, he's comin' down here. I already done told him. What's got Paddy all riled up? Looked like steam was coming out of his ears."

Listening as Maeve explained, with her pleasing Irish lilt, what was going on at the pub, I found myself picking up on the Southern drawl Winnie used.

"Some folks, I tell ya. Can't believe he's gettin' mixed up in these small-town politics. You'd think this here town would welcome some outside influence like it always has. Greeks, Irish, Germans, you name it. They say us Southerners move as slow as molasses, but that's not the case with this situation, no sir. It's somethin' else entirely.

"If you ask me, it seems like y'all are getting the runaround because you're bringing some competition to local restaurants. 'Cept with all that strange foreign stuff you folk like to make, I'm not so sure. But putting that aside, there's plenty of business to go around here, what with the snowbirds landing and all them tourists who keep finding us year after year. People just get stuck in their own little bubble sometimes. Don't you worry none. Nice to meet you again, Katie." And with that, Winnie turned and disappeared back between the bushes and flower beds she'd come from.

Maeve waved me into the house. "Come along, Katie. After your walk, maybe you'd like some sweet tea. But then you might need something stronger after meeting Winnie. She's a force of nature but a good neighbor. She likes to say she feels the pulse of the neighborhood, and I think she might be right. Seems to know what's going on all over Seaside."

"What are snowbirds?" I asked.

"They are the retired people who travel south for the winter." Maeve pulled out her ever-present glass jug of sweet tea from the refrigerator.

"Do you think she's right about it being small-town issues and not construction problems that are stalling the opening?"

Maeve shrugged. "Could be a wee bit of both. I'm staying optimistic that we can open Wednesday."

My taste for sweet tea was still evolving, but I accepted the glassful that Maeve put on the kitchen table for me.

"I'm thinking I'd like to include some traditional Southern appetizers for the opening, along with a few Irish samples," Maeve said.

I chuckled. "Not all that strange foreign stuff Winnie mentioned?"

"Right. But she had a point that I've also considered. First off, the Irish culinary world of appetizers, or as we call them, starters, is slim. And regardless of what Winnie thinks, we're more the hearty fare type. Thick soups. Meat and potatoes. By putting out some familiar local food, our guests will not go away hungry."

She made total sense. The vibe of the Irish pubs as a sanctuary from every day cares goes well beyond the food served there. And if some people here feel like Winnie suggested, they might appreciate a mixed menu. "That's not a bad idea at all," I said. "And you are right to ingratiate yourself with the locals any way you can."

"Tell me what you think about this." Maeve reached for a cookbook from the shelf. "The local women's group takes members' recipes and puts them in this book. They use the sales as a way to raise funds to help the community. What about if I put some of their favorites on a rotating menu? Like..." She began opening to pages tabbed with small sticky notes. She stopped and spun the book for me to see. The recipe she pointed to was for fried okra. "And I can sell this book in our little gift area. We've gotten so much encouragement over these many months, and I want to make everyone feel welcome."

"What other things do you have planned for the opening?"

"Now that you're back, I was hoping you'd have some more ideas. Throwing parties is not my forte. But it is yours." She reached to take my hand. "You have got to stay longer. Please. We really could use not only the family support you bring, but your talent too. Let me show you the folder of what I've decided on. It's sparse, but I'm sure you'll have some more ideas." She left me at the kitchen table.

Here I'd been feeling I came for their support, which I received in full measure. Maybe helping with the opening party was a way to pay them back for all they'd given me when I ran away from LA. No, it would be better if I treated it as taking a sabbatical.

Maeve returned with a spiral notebook. "The dollar store had all sorts of colors. I picked out a green one because I thought it would be good luck." She opened the cover to reveal lined sheets with carefully penciled words on them. She flipped pages over, licking her finger every so often, until she came to what she'd been looking for, then moved the Seaside Cove Woman's Club cookbook aside to make room for her notebook.

"These pages are the food ideas for the opening party. We want everything food-wise to be free that day. And…" She leaned over to flip the page to the next one. "These are some of our menu items that we'll be offering to taste that day."

"Looks good." I skimmed over the dishes she'd listed. "I'm looking forward to trying these. But what is it I can help with?"

"Can you work up something to dress the place up without a lot of expense?" Maeve's shoulders slumped as she let out a long breath. "We're already way over our budget with all the problems during construction."

"Could you cut back on the food? Or charge a token amount?"

"We've talked about giving out drink tickets. Maybe like you get two free drinks, then pay after that."

"That's not a bad idea. I imagine the beer will be flowing that day. After all, it's a very Irish thing, but you don't want people driving drunk. Even if it is only their golf cart."

"Right, Katie, our thoughts exactly. Besides some decorations, and stuff like that, could you stop in at the newspaper office with me tomorrow? Hannah's holding off on any announcement, what with the delays. And I thought maybe you would have more of an idea of what it should look like. You must see so many styles of invitations."

"I'd be happy to go with you," I said. "And by the way, do you have a Facebook page yet?"

"Oh goodness no! I'm just learning how to email and text. All that social media malarkey is beyond me."

"Do you mind if I set one up? It's one way people find businesses. You could promote all the good things happening at Paddy's Pub. I think it would be a great marketing tool."

"If you say so. But you know what this means?" Maeve's sly grin confused me.

What was she getting at?

"It means that you'll have to stay to manage this face page!" She dramatically flung her hands in the air. "Heaven knows I have my plate full."

Then, with another cute little grin, she began picking up our dishes. "And it means you'll be here to join my book club! We're meeting on Thursday night. You should come along. Oh, and you must remember my sewing circle. Would that be something you'd enjoy too?"

I'd play her at her own game. Glancing down and casually flipping one of her notebook pages, I said, "Oh, no, it doesn't matter if I live here. I can manage your social media from Los Angeles. I'm sure I can get your staff to take photos and send them to me. No problem. I'll get it set up tonight, making myself the administrator. This will be fun!" I saw her fake pout. "But if I'm still in town I'd enjoy going with you to your book club on Thursday."

Then, with a quick hug goodnight, I went to my bedroom and fired up my laptop. I had a few tasks to do in order to get the Paddy's Pub Facebook page ready for launch. I created an online list of what needed to be done. Who designed their logo? I would need to get files from him. And get a clean copy of the menu from the printer. I hadn't seen the website design, but I hoped I could obtain colors and fonts that would work with the branding they were using. It made me chuckle to think about how different opening a pub would have looked even twenty years ago, before the advent of social media. After searching through other Facebook business pages here in Seaside Cove, there seemed to be quite a mix of styles.

It wasn't long before I found myself checking out Irish-focused businesses on the panhandle and came across musicians. Could we manage to get even one lone fiddle player this late in the game?

I'd closed my laptop and was dozing off when I heard Paddy come home. Turning over and curling further under Maeve's quilt, I slept.

CHAPTER FOUR

"You're now on Facebook!" I announced as I poured myself a cup of morning coffee.

"Hear that, Paddy? Our business is on social media. We are part of the great big worldwide net!" Maeve hugged her husband from behind as he sat bent over his coffee cup.

"Web, Maeve. It's called the World Wide Web. Isn't that what the website we've paid good money for does?" he mumbled as he took a sip of coffee.

"The website is an important part of starting a business now, but it's set up to be more static," I said, walking over to join him at the table. "Social media is more fluid. If someone searches for Paddy's Pub, it will show up on both your website and social media. But with social media, you can run ads, update content, and interact with people."

"I'll bet searching for Paddy's Pubs brings up the hundreds of them around the world. Not the one here in Seaside." He pushed himself away from the table. "The one that's not even open. But that name, despite it being common, had always been a part of my dream. Enough talk. This old Irish fool has work to do."

"Ah now, cut it out, will ya? Yes, you may be old, but you are no fool. Everything will work out. Just look at this beautiful day. The sun is shining. The birds are singing."

Paddy embraced Maeve. "This is true, my sweet lass."

I watched Maeve's eyes close as she sank into Paddy, soaking up the moment. Would that I find that sort of love one day. I must have let out a big sigh because they both turned to me.

"Is something wrong, Katie dear?" Maeve said, pulling herself away.

"No, I'm fine. How'd last night go, Paddy? Did you get things straightened out and locked up tight?"

With a faraway look, he said, "I believe I did. I'll confirm that this morning. Keep your fingers crossed that we get our occupancy permit today, like the building inspector promised. Then we still need a resolution about the parking problem."

Maeve's eyes snapped open with surprise. "I didn't know there was a problem with that. Who can okay it?"

"The town council. They meet Monday night. But nothing will get done if I don't get meself over there now. What are you two up to today?"

"We are heading over to the Gazette. I want Katie to see the ad we'll be running. Katie has agreed to help us with a few things to get ready for the opening."

"Hope you're okay with that, Uncle Paddy. It's what I'm good at, setting up and running parties. While I'm here, I'd be happy to help wherever I can."

"Then we'll come by the place," Maeve continued. "Katie hasn't seen all we've accomplished since she got back. Now run along Paddy. The day won't wait for us with this dallying around."

Winnie, wearing a wide-brimmed straw hat and perched on a three-legged stool in one of her flower gardens, hollered out a morning greeting as Maeve and I left. We headed toward our first stop, the offices of Seaside Cove's newspaper. Maeve filled me in, explaining that the print copy of the paper came out twice weekly but that the online site was updating constantly. She told me that the editor was the granddaughter of the paper's founder and had only recently taken over from her own father.

The young secretary at the front waved us on

through to the editor's back office, where Hannah greeted us warmly. "Take a load off, Maeve. And nice to meet you, Katie. Are you enjoying your Florida visit?"

"Sure am. It's been wonderful to be with family. Plus, I'm relishing the peacefulness and slower pace of small-town life."

Hannah laughed easily. "Some think we Southerners move too slow, but I know what you mean. Now, Maeve, what can I help you with?"

Maeve raised her hopeful, crisscrossed fingers. "I have a date to use for our opening. Though things are still dragging out. Paddy's about to pull out his hair over this entire mess."

"Least he has a full head of hair to begin with. Greg's losing his hair. Starting from a less than stellar head of hair to begin with, it's not pretty." Hannah pulled out a pad to make notes on. "So, what's the date you want me to plug in?"

"We're shooting for Wednesday. But I should be able to confirm after the town council meeting on Monday. Paddy's dealing with some parking problem. Hannah, could you pull up the ad we have worked out and let Katie take a peek at it? She's going to do a few things for us while she's in town, and I want to give her a chance to see it."

Hannah reached for her laptop, but I said, "If you

could just send me the file, I'd appreciate that. Here's my email." I handed her one of my business cards. "That way, I'll not waste your time now and will be able to take a look at it later. I've set up a Facebook page, so at a minimum, we'll add that information."

Hannah glanced at the card. "Party planner? What an interesting profession. If you're familiar with the program we use, you can go in and make the updates yourself. Otherwise, return to me, and I'll get it to the staff. I've been planning on attending the opening of course, but I'd like to do an advance article about it. Would it work to come over later today so I can get a short interview and take a few photos?"

Maeve and I looked at each other. I knew she was concerned about Paddy's frame of mind. Did he need one more thing to add to his list?

Hannah continued, "It would build more excitement and get more eyeballs than an ad alone will. Though I appreciate you buying an advertisement. It's the ads that financially support our business."

Maeve took a deep gulp before saying, "Sure, Hannah. That would be wonderful. I can't commit to Paddy's availability, but I would think he could make a little time for you. We're heading over right now."

Hannah nodded. "I promise I won't take much time.

Katie, you'll find the layout of the advertisement in your email box shortly."

This was my first return to the pub since before Christmas. I was surprised by how much had gotten done since I left. The interior was warm and welcoming. Smells of freshly brewed coffee came from the small coffee area to the right, where Paddy sat talking with a man he introduced as his insurance agent. Sturdy stoneware mugs lined dark wood shelving. Maeve briefly explained their plans to personalize mugs for regular customers of what she called the Coffee Corner.

On the other side of the entry area was the pub and restaurant. The walls were partially covered by dark wooden panels, and the remaining wall space was painted a deep, rich color and adorned with frames holding portraits of famous Irish writers and musicians, as well as traditional Irish artwork. The bar and restaurant space were softly illuminated by stained glass lamps and elegant wall sconces, casting a warm golden hue throughout the room. The bar itself was crafted from dark mahogany and featured a brass footrail. Behind it, brass taps stood ready for use while rows of gleaming pint glasses sat waiting to be filled. The shelves were lined with an assortment of bottles. I noted many Irish whiskies among them.

Wooden tables and chairs dotted the cozy space, along with various elevated booths and intimate snugs, small private seating areas often found in Irish pubs. A small fireplace in one corner was surrounded by comfortable armchairs for patrons to relax in, and tucked away in another corner was a small stage. The air was filled with the comforting smell of wood and leather.

Hannah popped in just as the insurance agent was leaving. Paddy and Maeve took a few minutes to talk with her while I strolled around checking out the photographs of Ireland hanging throughout. When the interview was finished, Hannah waved goodbye and walked out with Maeve, who had announced she needed to make a grocery store run.

As soon as they were out of earshot, Paddy asked if I'd like to see how the second-floor rooms were looking. He most definitely was in a more upbeat frame of mind. My jovial Irish uncle was back. Following him up the broad staircase, I noticed the rich woodwork. How authentic it made the entire place feel! This banister must have been original to the bank. It felt like it had been here for decades as the well-preserved finish was smooth under my hand.

"Remember when you were here before, and I showed you the hurricane strap issue in the copper ceiling?" Paddy asked.

"Vaguely. I'm not into construction terms, but I remember the copper panel had been removed. Something up under it needed to be brought up to code?"

With a nod, he said, "Roger, my general contractor, finally got that resolved. Which meant more money spent, but with the weather around here, it probably was important. But meeting all the codes and regulations is exhausting."

"Did a part of you wonder how this building withstood hurricanes prior to you stepping in?"

"Aye, that did cross me mind. But what's that expression? You can't fight City Hall."

"That's it. What was the parking lot issue you mentioned this morning? I hope you don't have another fight on your hands."

Paddy motioned for me to follow him back toward his second-floor office in the rear of the building. From his window, I took in the breathtaking view of the Wimico River, and the expansive nature preserve across on the other side. The building was strategically placed higher than the river, preventing any potential flooding. Directly below us was a spacious parking lot available for customers to enter through the back entrance.

Down below, I saw the refrigerated trailers brought in to keep perishables safe until the electrical issues were resolved.

"This is a beautiful view. What's the issue with parking? There are lots of empty spaces back here," I said.

"You're right. With me original plan to just use the first floor, we were grand. But when I realized the old lift works dandy, I knew I wanted to make use of areas on the second floor as well. Unfortunately, that opened up a whole lot of trouble for us."

While Paddy continued to explain the details of his plan to appease the city council members, a man angrily stormed toward an old blue pickup truck parked in the lot below us. His hand slammed against the hood as he retrieved a pack of cigarettes from his front shirt pocket and tapped it against his palm in a sharp gesture. As someone who never smoked, I didn't understand why he hit the pack against his palm. Was it meant to pack the tobacco tighter? But his actions seemed to convey a deep anger and frustration. He was not happy.

"Looks like Rooster has hit another snag," Paddy said, watching over my shoulder. A new shiny white van with Baker Electrical Contractors painted on it took a fast turn and pulled up alongside Rooster's pickup.

"Here I thought they had it all figured out." Paddy sounded so deflated. "But based on what I'm observing, there are still some electrical problems. My general contractor said that Sammy Baker was the best commercial electrical contractor available. All I heard was the word best. Should have paid more attention to the next word…available."

Across River Road, the people going into Gator's for lunch turned to check out the raised voices coming from Paddy's parking lot.

"Beggin' your pardon, Katie. I'll be heading below to sort out the commotion. The electrical work is the last building issue holding up this project. It better be done and ready for approval. Roger has a big meeting sched-uled with Tim Douglas, the bigwig at the buildin' department, tomorrow night. Tim's none too pleased about a weekend evening meeting, but he's agreed to it and I can't be wasting his time now, can I? And on top of that, I need to sort out these electrical issues before my lease for them two trailers outside expires. Renting 'em for any longer would cost me hundreds more. Money I simply don't have."

CHAPTER FIVE

To ease Paddy's agitation, Maeve and I had taken him on a walk after dinner last night. He had been upset when he found out that Rooster, the man with the old pickup, was ordered to leave the job at Paddy's due to a supposed emergency at the Fulton Inn restaurant. Sammy, Rooster's boss, promised Paddy that the problems at the pub were under control and that electricians would be back on site tomorrow. Paddy fumed with anger.

"No extra charge, he goes! Why he'd better not charge me any more than the contract price. None of this has been by fault of mine," Paddy said.

I didn't want to even ask if he'd still open by Wednesday but Maeve did it for me. Uncle Paddy had a quick answer for her. "If we don't, someone is going to have to pay. So help me god I'm ready to strangle whoever is behind all this."

"Paddy, stop that nonsense. Emergencies happen. I'm sure the Bayview restaurant didn't want to have to deal with electrical problems and get a big bill either," Maeve said.

"Ah but tell me, who owns the place?"

"The mayor's wife, I think. What does that have to do with it?"

Paddy turned red in his face and clenched his jaw. "It better have nothing to do with it."

Maeve gave me a sorry-about-all-this look over her shoulder before taking Paddy's hand in hers and saying, "It's looking like another beautiful sunset over the Gulf. Shall we walk down to the fishing pier?"

This morning, Paddy appeared to be in better spirits. After making plans to go out to eat at the Rum Runner later in the day, he left in his golf cart to make sure Sammy and Rooster were back at work at the pub. He wanted everything ready for the meeting with the building inspector and Roger, his general contractor, later today.

My morning was spent on the comfy front porch

swing brainstorming ideas for social media marketing of Paddy's Pub and its grand opening. After grabbing an iced sweet tea and plumping the floral pillows into a backrest, I put my feet up and nestled into the corner of the swing.

I created a spreadsheet on my laptop and began filling it with the limited data I had so far. Being a Virgo meant I craved organization and felt satisfaction in putting things down in written form. I knew I needed both my left-brain logic and analytical skills, as well as my right brain's creative abilities, to make this project a success.

I needed more photos of the inviting interior as I'm sure it would attract customers. Paddy and Maeve's personalities would also be integral in making the place a success. Inspired by Paddy's vision, I decided to feature his words that this wasn't a typical new restaurant or bar, it was a public house, on the cover photo for Facebook. And of course, I made sure to highlight the inviting Coffee Corner where the Murphy family welcomed everyone to relax, read the newspaper, or play a game of cribbage.

Hannah's ad for the Gazette was okay, but a photograph of Maeve and Paddy together would really draw people's eyes to it. Here too, I needed more photographs to catch people's attention. Oh, I know! Maeve said she wanted to go to the Rum Runner on Horseshoe Island for the oyster special tonight. We might time it to catch the setting sun at just the right angle. The logo they'd had the web designer create was really very good and should appear in the ad too.

Their budget for the opening had been cut back. Maeve explained how the construction cost overruns ate into the party they'd hoped to throw. Still down the rabbit hole I went, searching for Irish musicians. YouTube videos were super helpful. I was lost in watching performances of musicians in the area.

The rhythmic beat of the Bokharan drum and the enchanting melodies of the Uilleann pipes coming out of my laptop must have caught Winnie's ear. I burst out laughing when she appeared doing an Irish jig.

"You know that America's bluegrass music can be traced back to Irish immigrants coming to America," she said as she joined me on the porch.

"I didn't know that, but listening to it now, I see the connection," I said. "You do a pretty authentic jig."

"I'm no spring chick, but I still have enough spring in my step to pull it off."

Together we listened to sample recordings of musicians, and between availability and price, I decided on a group I wanted to contact. The Sheehans were a husband and wife duo. She played the Irish fiddle and her husband the Bodhran and tin whistle. They both sang as well. Luckily had availability for Wednesday.

Winnie applauded my choice. I started another video of the Sheehans and cranked up the sound. At that point, Maeve poked her head out the door. "What on earth is going on?"

Winnie grabbed her and pulled her out to the front porch.

"I've been putting on a show tryin' to do an Irish jig, but I reckon you can show us how it's really done."

Maeve discreetly raised her skirt and, with a few flicks and kicks, demonstrated her jig for us. "Who's that you have playing? I like their sound."

"It's the Sheehan duo. And if all goes well, they will play at your grand opening!" I told her excitedly.

"Now Katie. We can't afford live musicians. Too much has been spent already."

"It's my gift to thank you for taking me in and cheering me up. I didn't know what I could do to show my appreciation. But I hope this will do it."

"Are you sure Katie? You know you're family, and we always help family. You are a blessing to us just being here."

"Well then consider it family help," I said. "Now it would help me if you'd approve the changes I made to the newspaper ad and this flyer I'm going to post around town. I notice that several of the shops on Main Street allow advertisements to be put up in their windows."

Maeve reached in her apron pocket for her reading glasses. "That sounds great, Katie. Thank you."

"Y'all got any notion how many folks will be there? I'm bringing my church ladies, bless their hearts, and their husbands. And the farmer I buy eggs from and the doctor what treats the dang bursitis in my knees. Then there's that traveling hairdresser who comes round the old age home."

"Grand, Winnie," Maeve said. "Thanks a million! I know Paddy's gang of old-timers will show up for the grand opening all right. And my quilting mates and book club ladies can't wait to see what we've done with the place. The whole area is glad to see us bring that eyesore back to its original glory."

"It was a mighty task, but you two nailed it, like taking out the boarded-up second-story windows and cleaning the exterior. Lordy, but that place had been let go," Winnie said.

"Does Paddy have fishing friends? Wouldn't they want to come?" I asked.

"You're right Katie. In fact, one of those posters should go up at the Up River Lodge. Oh, and the marina." Maeve looked at her watch. "Oh, my goodness. We'd better get going. It took some convincing on my part to get Paddy to agree to go to the island for dinner. I don't want to keep him waiting."

As Winnie was leaving, she called back to me. "I'll help put flyers up. I know this town like the back of my hand."

"Appreciate that," Maeve called after her.

CHAPTER SIX

Paddy came walking out to our car looking very happy. It was a relief to see him looking so jovial. Things must have gone well with the electrical work today. But before he got to the car, Rooster pulled Paddy aside and told him something. I watched Paddy's relaxed expression turn to concern in an instant. His fingers curled into fists as he approached us.

I don't think Maeve witnessed his mood change. She greeted him cheerfully. "Hi my sweet. How was your day?"

Paddy let out a frustrated grunt. "Everything was going smoothly until that." He motioned toward Rooster, who had just returned inside the building.

"What did he say?"

Paddy brushed off her question with an incoherent mumble.

"So things are stalled again?" I asked. Being on the periphery of all that was going on, I didn't know if it was my place to get involved at all. But with my own business, I didn't have anyone to bounce business issues off, and I later learned it would have helped me to discuss these things.

"Roger, my general contractor, seemed certain he had everything under control and the final issues with the electricity would be fixed so our electrical inspection will clear tonight. That was one big box to check off. Then I convinced one of the council members who owns the souvenir shop down the street to stop in and look over what I'd pulled together for the meeting about the parking issue tomorrow night. He seemed to get a good sense of what I was proposing and agreed it looked like something the others will approve of."

"Well, that all sounds lovely. So why the long face?" Maeve pulled her car out onto the street and headed toward the causeway ahead. "Or do you just want to get out to the beach and enjoy dinner at Rum Runners?"

Paddy reached over to gently rub her shoulder. It brought a smile to her lips. He glanced at me in the back seat. "You're making a good point, my darlin'. I'll let all me long face go and enjoy my lovely company."

This unseasonably warm weather felt wonderful on my skin. The humidity from the Gulf of Mexico had caused my hair to become unruly, but I didn't mind. The long, winding causeway stretched over the water, disappearing into the island ahead. Breathing in the salty air left me feeling relaxed. I hadn't been out to the island, named after the Gulf of Mexico's horseshoe crab, since I'd gotten back from Wisconsin. I'd imagined I'd be lying on the beach reading my new E.L. Brooks book by now, but more important things had needed doing.

The sun was setting on the horizon, casting a warm golden light over the glistening water below. Small boats sailed lazily by. In the distance, I saw a cluster of beach houses standing tall on stilts, their pastel colors blending into the landscape. As we got closer, I noticed people strolling along the shore, silhouetted against the orange and pink hues of the setting sun.

The tall, muscular man who greeted us at Rum Runners could have come straight from a California beach town, so when he said, "It's been too long my friends and fellow cheeseheads," I was totally caught off guard.

"Looking like this will be another Packers' season without a spot in the playoffs."

"But there is always next year," Maeve chimed in. "Tyler Berman, I'd like you to meet my niece, Katie

Murphy. She's been visiting us from her home in Los Angeles."

"Katie, it's a pleasure," Tyler extended his hand across the bar. "It's been nice to meet other transplants from my home state of Wisconsin. I grew up in Madison. In fact, we get quite a few snowbirds from the upper Midwest here in our little paradise. But few Californians like yourself. So welcome! What can I get you?"

"Do you have a specialty drink you can suggest? And one that would pair with the oysters we're having tonight?" Ouch, that sounded so Californian even to my ears, but this handsome hunk of a man had thrown me off guard.

"Pair with? I don't know about that," he said with a wink. "But in my mind, nothing beats the classic margarita for getting in a beach frame of mind."

I'd not had a margarita in ages. In fact, I didn't do much drinking because most parties I went to were ones where I was working. And wine is so big in California that it was the easiest thing to reach for. But right now, the thought of an icy margarita with a salted rim made me smile. Paddy and Maeve both had one as well, which surprised and pleased me.

We chose a table near the expanse of beach that led to the waters lapping over the white sand. Children played at building sandcastles, and in the distance, seagulls swooped and danced in the air, their cries echoing across the landscape. A few souls even braved the chill of the evening to take a dip in the ocean.

This would be the perfect time to get some photos of Paddy and Maeve for publicity and social media. This glorious glow wouldn't last long. I convinced them to walk with me to the shoreline. Angling them just right so they weren't squinting against the sun, I captured at least a dozen photographs of them. When they began walking back to the table hand in hand, I snapped a few more.

Our raw oyster and mixed seafood platter waited for us when we returned to our table.

Paddy couldn't believe I'd never eaten raw oysters. "I'm amazed you never had any when you lived back home in Ireland. Especially since many of our family lived in the Galway area where some of the very best oysters are harvested."

"I was a fussy eater, so that limited what I ate or even tried. And it certainly didn't include raw seafood," I laughed. "But since being here in America I've grown to like sushi. Though for some reason not tried these up to this point."

"Well then, here's to your first time!" Tyler appeared next to our table. "Do you know what they say about these beauties?"

Maeve blushed and ducked her eyes, while Paddy choked back a laugh before saying, "Now Tyler, we're in mixed company!"

"I think Katie might appreciate knowing the possible benefits," Tyler said with a wink in Paddy's direction.

"What is going on here?" I said, looking first at Maeve and then at Paddy. "Are you setting me up for a joke?"

"No. It's just an old tale that oysters are an aphrodisiac," Paddy practically choked on the last word.

"Oh my!" Tyler covered his mouth with his fingers in mock embarrassment. "I wouldn't have brought that up in front of these ladies. I wanted Katie to know they are loaded with vitamin D."

Paddy let out a hearty chuckle. "Ah sure, now I've gone and put me foot in me mouth, haven't I? Don't be going back to Ireland telling them your dear ol' uncle was leading you astray here in the States."

I reached over and patted Paddy's hand. "No worries. It'll be our little secret. But now, please, someone tell me how I'm supposed to eat these slimy-looking things and get all that healthy vitamin D."

"Let me help with that," Tyler said, sitting down next to me. He picked out one of the rough, jagged-edged shells from the bed of ice. "As you bring the oyster to your nose, you may detect a slight scent of seaweed, as well as a tangy, salty aroma."

He raised the oyster up to my nose and I inhaled.

"I like to think it smells like a fresh ocean breeze on a warm summer day," he said. "Would you like me to show you how to eat it?"

"I think that might be good," I said, trying to avoid looking directly at the grayish-brown blob I would be eating.

Tyler brought the shell up to his mouth. "You put your lips against the cool, smooth surface of the oyster as you tilt your head back and let it slide into your mouth. The fluid sloshes gently against your lips. The first flavor might be the briny, salty ocean water that the oyster was harvested from. But the flavors will evolve as you chew."

And with that, the oyster slid between his lips. He slowly closed his eyes and his strong square jaw rhythmically chewed. With a quiet sigh, he opened his eyes. "Easy peasy," he said. "Your turn. But be sure to savor the experience."

Figuring I'd skip the savoring for another time, I let the slimy thing just slide right down my throat.

"How was it?" Maeve asked.

As I quickly reached for one of the grilled oysters

that sat on the seafood platter, I said, "I think it might be an acquired taste."

"Always good to try new things, though," Tyler said, giving me a thumbs up. "Paddy, I've been waiting for an invitation to your grand opening. You didn't go and have one without me, did you?"

"No chance. We need all the support we can muster," Paddy said.

Maeve reached out to rest her hand on Paddy's. "There have been a few hiccups, but I can feel it's going to happen very soon."

"Will you be in town for it?" Tyler asked me.

"I will. I've extended my stay and arranged to work from here for a while longer. That way, I can help with the opening."

"That's good to hear." He paused and held my eyes a moment before adding, "I mean the part about helping them out."

"We're so proud of Katie," Maeve said. "She moved from Ireland years ago and now has a successful party planning business in LA. Movie stars, Hollywood executives, politicians. All the big fancy mansions and lawns. You should see the events she puts together. Money is no concern to those people."

"But it is to us," Paddy mumbled. "I've had such

construction overruns and unforeseen expenses. We are glad you can stay longer and hope it doesn't cut into your business in California. I also want you to know that we don't have much money left to put toward the opening."

"I know, Paddy. Maeve has kept me informed. But I've set up lots of free publicity using Facebook and Instagram. That's part of why I took the photographs tonight."

Tyler nodded and smiled at me before turning toward Paddy. "She's right. Not all publicity costs money. And congrats to you, Katie, on building a business in a tough market like LA. I follow Paddy's Pub on social media. You'll announce details of the opening there?"

"Yes. And I'll be printing flyers as soon as the details are finalized. Can we post it here on the island?"

"Absolutely. To save time, you could send me the PDF file. I can print it off my computer and distribute it here."

"That would be much appreciated."

Tyler and I quickly exchanged email and phone information. I must admit I'd wished we could have lingered longer, but that didn't happen.

Paddy got a text that left him with a puzzled expression. He looked up and said, "As much as it pains me to depart from all of this, duty is calling. If you fine lasses wouldn't mind dropping me off at the pub, I have some pressing matters to attend to."

CHAPTER SEVEN

The loud knocking on my door startled me from my sleep. I blinked to clear my eyes. It was still dark out, and it wasn't yet morning, so I hadn't overslept. Maeve opened the door. She was still in her nightgown with an open robe over her shoulders. I sat up and swung my legs from under the covers to the cold floor.

"What is it?"

"Katie, a call has come in that there's trouble at the pub. Can you go with Paddy? He's almost dressed. I hate to ask this of you, but I'm so worried."

A phone rang somewhere in the house, and I heard Paddy's voice, but I couldn't make out the words.

I shook my head to clear it as I tapped the screen of my phone to see the time. 4:59 AM. My first thought

48

was a fire because of the difficulty they'd been having with the electrical. That would be awful.

"Please hurry. The police are at the pub." She pulled my window curtain aside to peer outside. "He's getting into the golf cart." She pounded on the window and held up a finger for him to wait a minute, but he didn't see her.

"Look, I'll get dressed and drive over to see what's going on. Maybe they didn't lock up again and someone got inside." Maeve's face was pinched and she nervously rubbed her fingers. "Is there something else I should know?"

She bit her lip before saying, "No. But Katie, I have a bad feeling. Please hurry."

Within a few minutes, I pulled up to the front of the pub where Paddy's golf cart, three police cars, and an ambulance were parked. The door was open and I let myself in, walking toward the bar area ahead. Paddy saw me and hurried over, demanding to know what I was doing here.

"Maeve sent me. She was worried because you didn't explain what the call was about."

"Give me a minute. I'll be right back."

A sobbing woman sat on the bottom step of the large front staircase. What was going on? Others, including police officers, were gathered around her. Had she been hurt? Maybe fallen on the stairs? I moved in closer and between the legs of the people gathered, I saw a small dog sitting at attention next to someone sprawled on the pub floor.

Then I noticed Hannah taking in the scene and asked, "Hannah, what is this? Who is that man? Is he okay?"

She shook her head. "Far from it. He's deceased."

I recoiled with shock.

"Looks like Mayor Trimble may have fallen down the staircase and been here for hours. That woman crying is his wife, and her brother is around here somewhere too. And that little cutie is his dog, Tootsie."

"The mayor? Why would he have been here?"

Hannah shrugged. "That's what the police are asking your uncle about."

No wonder Paddy took off so suddenly earlier. My heart sank for him. After all he'd gotten through these past weeks, a dead body shows up in his business. I couldn't have ever imagined something like this happening here in Seaside Cove. "Who found him?"

"I don't know yet," Hannah said before leaning in to whisper, "His wife said he had a couple of important issues to take care of and left the house after dinner last night. He's been known to deal with issues at the Salty Dawg."

Hannah switched gears when she saw who Paddy was talking to. "Hi, Chief. Heard this on my scanner. Anything you want to share with me? People will start making stuff up if you don't put out a statement. You know Vivian will be on the phone as soon as she leaves here. Word's gonna spread around fast. Don't leave me hanging with the headline 'Mayor Dead Under Mysterious Circumstances.'"

The chief chuckled. "Now Hannah, no need for a headline just yet. How about you wait until the doctor gives me his opinion? As to what his wife wants to say, I can't let that dictate the speed of my investigation."

Paddy didn't introduce me to the Chief of Police but stepped back and said, "Sorry I took off without an explanation."

As a police officer walked nearby, the chief asked him to tape off the scene.

"Is that really necessary?" Paddy asked.

"You of all people should know we need to protect the scene until we can determine why he was here and if this is an accident."

"Of course. You're right," Paddy said. "It's just that I've scheduled our opening party for Wednesday. Will we be able to keep those plans?"

"Day after tomorrow? I can't promise you that. I'd suggest you postpone it. I'll do my best, but until we know what he died from, I need to secure the scene. It's possible this wasn't an accident. There's a chance he was involved in an altercation."

"Possible he was murdered, you mean," Paddy said glumly.

As a former Chief of Police himself, Paddy grasped the situation. Someone was in this place for an unknown reason late at night and died here. Even I got the jest of that and could understand not jumping to a conclusion.

We all heard a remark that Mayor Trimble might have been here taste-testing the Guinness. The chief spun sharply to see the person who had spoken. "There will be none of that commentary or you'll be sitting behind the desk for the next month. I'm sure Blaire would welcome the chance for some time in the field. She'd gladly trade places with you."

"Sorry, sir. That was unprofessional."

"Now you think so, huh?"

"It won't happen again."

"See that it doesn't."

Paddy led me away from the scene. Already at this early hour, cars were out on the street, slowing down to see inside and find out what was going on.

"Is there something I can do to help Paddy?"

"No, Katie. You shouldn't have come."

"You know you should give Maeve more credit. Worrying about things and thinking you're not telling her everything can be worse than the truth."

"Of course. I'll call and let her know what has happened," he said.

"What did happen? A horrible accident?"

"I don't know Katie. It doesn't make sense. Sammy and Tim met here last night. I caught up with them when you and Maeve dropped me off. I needed to explain to the building inspector about the delay with the final electrical work. I wanted to be sure to push for the occupancy permit to be issued."

"I thought I heard you leave the house again later last night. Was Mayor Trimble here then?"

"I didn't see him." He avoided making direct eye contact as if he were keeping something hidden.

"Why did you go back to the pub again? And why so late?"

"You should just go home to Maeve now. The chief and I will handle this. I can't say much, but he knows about my past work in law enforcement. I'm sure he'll give me some information. Don't worry, Katie. It'll all work out." Paddy paused to take a deep breath and straighten his shoulders. "Katie, please just let Maeve know that the event is postponed again. But hey, how about we plan for Saturday instead? Saturday parties are always more fun than Wednesdays anyway, right?"

CHAPTER EIGHT

Stepping into my car, I took a moment to process what I had just witnessed. I was supposed to be here to celebrate the grand opening of my family's dream business. And yet, inside that building, there was a dead body. The police were taking over and my uncle was stymied yet again. Watching hours of CSI crime scene investigation shows did not prepare me for this reality. Those shows were scripted and fictional, unlike this real-life situation unfolding around me.

As I glanced over my shoulder to back out of my parking space, I caught sight of the river flowing into the bay. Life was going on despite the tragedy that had occurred. The town was waking up, with fishing boats and pleasure boats already on the water. Soon enough, the word would be spreading that the Mayor of Seaside Cove was dead.

The metallic knock startled me and I hit the brake. Had I backed into something?

Hannah called out, "Katie, wait."

I turned down my car window as soon as I realized it had been her knocking on my car hood. "You scared me."

She grimaced. "Sorry about that. But can I ask you something?" she said, sliding her sunglasses up.

"Sure. What is it?"

"I know your aunt and uncle will be disappointed about the opening being delayed again. You and Maeve seemed so certain of Wednesday and of course I get the reason for this delay. But do you have any idea why it had been delayed before?"

"Boy, Hannah, that's a tough one. But from what I gathered, it was just building and construction stuff." I looked around the parking area and was reminded of the parking issue. "And then there was a problem with the number of available parking spaces for bigger events, but Paddy seemed to think that will be resolved tonight by an idea he'd presented to one of the council members."

Hannah appeared to have listened carefully but I

sensed she was keeping something in check. What was she holding back? "Do you know more Hannah?"

She leaned in closer to my open window. "We are a small town, Katie. And even though Paddy and Maeve have been here a couple of years now, they are still considered newbies. I've heard some grumbling about Paddy opening this place. That he might be serious competition. Do you think the delays could be part of those rumors?"

"Competition? I don't know. But for who?" My eyes scanned along the waterfront. "All your places here seem so different. Gator's Seafood and Raw Oyster Bar? Hardly. The Salty Dawg…no way."

"How about the Bayview? Their special banquet space is limited. So when Paddy discovered the old elevator still functioned, and he decided to set up the second-floor rooms for banquets, things really changed, didn't they? No longer just another bar and grill sort of place, but an event venue," Hannah said.

"Where is the Bayview?"

"It's in the Fulton Inn. You've seen that, right? The pretty yellow building just up that way."

I remembered seeing it before and that Sammy and Rooster had to spend time there yesterday instead of at the pub. It was an eye-catching building.

"It belongs to the mayor's wife's family." With a

dramatic pause, Hannah snapped her sunglasses back down, covering her eyes.

"You're implying what?"

"I think there is more behind this than even the police know. Can we stay in touch? I'm going to do some further investigating myself."

"You'd make a good Mata Hari, Hannah. I'm heading home to talk with Maeve now and let her know what's up. On top of all of this, friends from Wisconsin are going to be in town this afternoon."

With a big wave, Hannah sashayed away in the direction of her office. I was left wondering if I should mention what she told me to Maeve. Nah, I'd better just stay out of the small-town intrigue for now. But instead of turning to head back to the cottage, I impulsively steered right to check out the Fulton Inn.

The inn was certainly an attractive historic landmark. Not much activity, but then it was Monday morning. So Mrs. Trimble owned this. Hmm...had her husband been purposely slowing down the pub's opening hoping Paddy's dream would die? Having seen the lengths people in Hollywood go to when they are worried about competition, I decided I shouldn't dismiss Hannah's suggestion too quickly. Entire love affairs were had over trying to knock another actor out of the way for a juicy role.

Through one of the porch windows I watched a waiter in a white shirt set a coffee pot down in front of a young couple. So that must be the restaurant area.

A horn blast behind me made me realize my gawking had caused me to drift out of my lane. The driver shook his fist at me and I gave him my best sorry 'bout that look as I maneuvered over toward the curb. The grass lawn around the inn could use a trim and I could use a hot coffee. Wonder if I can get one to go here? I decided to find out.

As soon as I stepped into the lobby of the historic inn, I felt as if I had been transported back in time. The grandeur of the late 1800s was still palpable in the high ceilings, ornate moldings, and intricate chandeliers that hung from above. The walls were adorned with vintage paintings and photographs of the hotel's early days. The faint scent of aged wood and a slight hint of mustiness wafted through the air, adding to the overall sense of history and age.

Behind the check-in desk stood a tired-looking receptionist. Her eyes lit up as she greeted me with a hopeful smile. Through a large cased opening to my right was the restaurant. It appeared deserted except for the couple I'd seen through the window. No waiter in sight. Ah well, I was sure Maeve would have coffee for me back at the house.

Just as I turned to leave, the front desk person asked, "Can I help you?"

"I'd like a coffee to go, but I don't want to trouble anyone. The waiter must be in back."

"Sorry for that ma'am. I suspect that's where he is," she mumbled. "Give me a moment." She walked into the restaurant and through a door that must lead to the kitchen, returning shortly with a paper cup in one hand and a lid in the other. "Cream? Sugar?"

"No. Black is good. Thanks. How much do I owe you?"

"On the house. Sorry you had to wait."

Over her shoulder, I saw the waiter scowling from the kitchen door. Okay, chill in the air here. More than a little tension in this place.

"Yoooo-hoooo! Katie!"

My eyes scanned the area I stood in. Who was calling my name?

"Oh Katie! Hold up there. I could use a little help." Winnie's easily identifiable frame turned the corner from a hall near the restaurant entrance.

"Winnie, what are you doing here?"

"Gotta grab some leftovers for the food bank. Usually there's a staff member who lends me a hand, but I couldn't find nobody. And there's a whole lotta stuff to load up in my van. Mind givin' me a hand?"

"Sure."

"Put your coffee down on that there brick propping the back door open and follow me this way to pick up the food."

As we began to move down the narrow hall, I heard a faint clanking of pots and pans in the kitchen and the gentle hum of the refrigerator running. The hallway had a distinct aroma of age, with the faintest hint of spices and cooking.

Through a swinging door, we entered another space where Winnie grunted as she bent to pick up a box. I grabbed the other one, which held bread and oversized cans of tomato sauce. Winnie pushed her backside against the swinging door, holding it open for me to navigate past her with my heavy load.

We put our boxes in with several others in the rear of Winnie's minivan. Winnie stood erect and arched her back, twisting side to side. "Well, thank ya, darlin'. Now what brings you round these parts? Thought you'd be lending a hand to Maeve and Paddy what with the opening in a few days. Or maybe you're just scooping out the competition? This place used to be the talk of the town, but times have changed. 'Course I don't come here often as a guest. It's a bit too fancy for my budget."

Quick thinking led me to hold up my coffee cup as an answer. But Winnie pinched her forehead and shot back. "Maeve makes a delicious cup of coffee. You're takin' the long way 'round the barn girl."

She had me on that astute observation. Oh well, word will get out soon, so I might as well tell her everything.

Winnie stood there, stunned, with her hands on her hips and her mouth hanging agape. For once, she was left without a comeback.

"I haven't told Maeve yet, so I'd better get going. Word will be spreading, and I don't want her to hear from someone else."

"Hold on there, missy. You can't just drop something like that then hurry off. And that don't explain why you are here at the Fulton."

"Well, um, I was driving by to see the place because Han…ah, someone, told me about it. And I thought I'd grab a nice hot coffee while I was here."

"Don't be trying to talk in circles child. Now tell me the truth."

I shared Hannah's thoughts with Winnie and observed her facial expression shift in front of me as if a light had suddenly turned on. She seemed to sense some truth in what I was saying.

"She's right to be suspicious. I've been doing this pantry run a long time and I hear things. You get on over to Maeve. I'll stop by for a quick minute before I go on with my pickups."

* * *

Maeve waited expectantly for me on her front porch swing, leaning forward when she saw me pull up.

I took a seat in one of the wicker porch chairs and took a long sip of my Bayview coffee. Taking a moment to put my mind to work on how to tell her, I decided the direct approach was best. "Paddy's fine, Maeve, but there's been a tragedy. The Mayor of Seaside Cove is dead."

"Oh no!" She gasped, clutching her hands to her chest. "Poor Mayor Trimble. Poor Vivian! I'll have to take a dish over to her."

"There's something else you should know. Paddy was called out this morning because Slim discovered Mayor Trimble's body at the bottom of the staircase in the pub."

"How on earth? Was it a heart attack? Or did he fall?"

Thankfully, Winnie arrived and took a seat next to Maeve. "Winnie, did you…"

"Know the mayor is dead?" Winnie asked. "I just learned it myself."

"But how'd you find out so soon?" Maeve asked.

"Ran into Katie on my food pantry pickup rounds.

She filled me in. I had to stop by and let you know how bad I feel about this."

"We all feel bad about Marvin's passing," Maeve patted Winnie's arm. "But that was sweet to stop."

Winnie's expression turned serious as she furrowed her brow and shook her head. "Didn't Katie tell you?" she asked. "The pub can't open anymore, not with that gaudy yellow crime scene tape strung up by the police."

Maeve's shoulders slumped and she held her head in her hands. "When will it ever open?"

"Not sure about when, but now the police are trying to figure out what was he doing there late at night. How did he get in?" I said.

"That old coot. Always poking his nose in everyone's business. He probably fell down the stairs. What in god's name was he doing there?" Winnie unexpectedly laughed out loud and slapped her knee. "Man loved his drink. Maybe he thought he'd get an early jump on this new pub and taste test the product. I'll bet Vivian was calling around to the bars looking for him. Wouldn't be the first time."

"It will be the last time now," I said. "And his poor wife was there when I arrived."

"I'll make up a batch of my sugared pecans to take to her, poor dear. She goes goofy for those," Winnie said.

"You mentioned something about things you heard

at the Bayview," I said, hoping to get more information from Winnie. She said Hannah was right to link the Bayview to what had been happening to Paddy's plans and maybe even a connection with the murder.

"I'll save that. Running behind." As Winnie rose from the swing, it released, and Maeve's feet lifted off the porch floor. "Now don't you fret, Maeve. This'll all take a day or two to settle. Paddy's Pub will open just fine. Though I suspect you might want to wait until after the funeral. Vivian will be sure to make a big deal out of that. Her social standing demands it. Lordy, this will be a big one."

I watched Winnie waddle back to her van and drive away.

"Sorry this happened to you and Paddy," I said.

Maeve kept her head tipped down, but her eyes looked up toward me.

"Maeve? What is it?"

Her chest expanded before she let out a deep exhale. "You didn't answer my question, Katie. Do they think it was a heart attack? Or an accident?"

"They don't know yet. I imagine the autopsy will answer that. Why?"

"Oh nothing. Just wondering. More coffee Katie? I'll make a fresh pot." She practically leaped out of the swing, sending it bouncing back and hitting her behind her knees. She steadied herself and scurried off inside the house.

Okay then. That was strange, but she's had a lot on her mind and this added one more thing to it.

The day seemed to drag by. Maeve tried distracting herself by keeping busy in the house. I took the time to explore more of Seaside Cove on foot, checking out the houseboats docked along the river and touring one of the historic mansions in town. I knew I'd stay for our visitors' arrival tomorrow, but beyond that, I wasn't sure. With the opening having to be postponed again and another date yet to be determined, the future was just so uncertain.

For all of us.

CHAPTER NINE

Tuesday morning broke bright and warm. Kenmare's front porch had a great view up and down past the other modest but beautifully kept cottages, creating a tableau of small-town life. A yellow school bus stopped down at the corner to pick up a group of five giggling girls. A woman in workout gear cycled by, waving when she saw me. A mailman, his pouch strapped across his chest, stood chatting with a neighbor down the street. Life was going on as normal for most everyone in Seaside Cove.

I couldn't help but think it would be a good distraction for us to have friends in town. Maeve and Paddy, who used to live in Harmony when he was Chief of Police there, knew Scott Drake and probably his new wife, Jackie Parker, the renowned photographer. I vaguely remember hearing that she had moved away, traveling the world with her photography. Perhaps she would be interested in displaying her work at our pub. I made a mental note to check if any local shops featured artists, as we could potentially do the same at our pub. With a working elevator, Paddy met accessibility requirements for hosting events upstairs, like craft fairs.

But, back to our company coming today. I knew Maeve was disappointed that now they would only get to take a peek inside the pub because of the yellow police tape. I hoped Paddy would be available to take them to the marina to check into a permanent docking space for Jack's boat. The four of them, Jackie and Scott Drake, along with his sister Sophia and her husband Jack, were booked to stay at the Fulton Inn. My visit yesterday showed me what a magnificent place it had once been, albeit a little rough around the edges now.

Inside the cottage, I found Maeve staring out the kitchen window. No doubt she'd had a lot dumped in her lap yesterday, what with the pub wrapped up in a death investigation. I didn't even want to think what the word murder attached to the scenario would mean.

It was just after noon when we spotted Jack and Sophia's boat motoring in our marina. I waved my hands high above my head. This would take their minds off the pub problems. The chief had told Paddy odds were he'd be able to get into the place on Thursday so the opening had already been rescheduled for Saturday after Paddy said any earlier would be too rushed feeling. I agreed with him wholeheartedly, having dealt with hurried party plans in my career and the memories of how hard it had been to keep them on the rails.

"Fella has a nice boat there," Paddy said, carefully watching the cabin cruiser slow as it passed the no-wake signs.

"It's so wonderful to have company from Wisconsin come to visit," Maeve said. "But I honestly only remember Scott Drake. The family lived outside of town. Didn't his father own a construction company, Paddy?"

"That's right. You know his sister and her husband too, don't you, Katie?" Paddy asked.

"I met them in Harmony over my Christmas visit. Sophia and Jack were in town for Jackie and Scott's wedding. They live in Tallahassee where Sophia is an event planner like me but on a corporate scale. I forget what her husband Jack does. They keep their boat docked up the coast, and I told them about what a great place Seaside Cove was, so they decided to travel here and check it out."

"That was sweet of you, Katie. I hope they like our little town," Maeve said.

"Oh, I just remembered something I didn't mention to you. There was a strange death in Harmony while I was there."

"Now that's a rarity," Paddy said. "I can't recall a murder in the entire time I was Chief of Police there."

"The woman who died was designing Jackie's wedding gown. What a twisted tale that was because this woman designed dresses for a soap opera that a client of mine acted in. And that client, Beverly, was also in Harmony for Jackie's wedding because she is her half-sister. Plus, hold on, one more degree of separation…it turns out that I'd met Jackie in Los Angeles when I was putting on a party there for Beverly, the soap opera actress, and Jackie was at the party because she was there in LA to look for wedding dresses."

"My head is spinnin' lass," Paddy said. "Don't ask me to repeat any of that back at you."

"Well now, isn't it a small world? But who is this Jackie other than a lucky woman for marrying Scott," Maeve asked.

"Her family had a photography studio in Harmony," I said.

"Oh, for goodness' sake. Is that Joanna and Bob's daughter? I remember them well. Joanna owned a dress shop on Main Street back in the day before the big department stores came along. I bought one or two dresses there. Joanna was so glamorous. Too bad about them dying so young."

"I met her aunt, Ruth Parker, at a winter festival that was going on," I said.

"Ruth Parker! A lovely woman. So, she's doing well then? You must remember her, Paddy. Ruth was running the studio when we left town. She must be in her eighties."

"I do remember Ruth. Her niece Jackie took over the studio recently." Paddy took Maeve's hand and smiled at me. "Our niece is a woman of the world now too. I don't think she'll stay here long with all that she has going on in California."

With the best shocked and sad look I could muster, I said, "Are you hinting I should leave?"

"Never ever! We want you to stay. You know you're like a daughter to us," Maeve said.

That tugged at my heartstrings. Maeve and Paddy never had children. Their relationships with the younger members of their family were so important to them. But eventually, I'd leave here because my life was on the West Coast, not the Gulf

Coast. But for now, I was happy for the break from my LA life.

When the Daniels' boat docked, we exchanged greetings and introductions before getting a tour of the craft. Paddy offered to take Jack to the marina office and introduce him to the owner. "I'll offer him a big discount at the pub if he finds a good spot for you and gives you a good rate," Paddy teased.

"I'd appreciate that," Jack said with a laugh. "And from what I've seen so far, this town looks great. We might even be able to afford a small second home, so we don't have to sleep on the boat for longer stays."

"Hold on there, young man. There's something you can do in return."

Jack grinned. "Ah, what would that be?"

Maeve swatted at Paddy. "Don't you be causing him no trouble. He'll be happy to set you up, Jack."

"Hold on woman, let me say my peace." He winked and turned to Jack, who was fighting back a big smile, trying to look serious.

"I hope I can give you what you want, Mr. Murphy."

"What I want in return is a deep-sea fishing trip. On our boat tour you pointed out how well set up your craft is for that."

Jack scratched his chin in contemplation. "Oh boy. I don't know about that, sir."

Sophia playfully punched his arm and he reached to hug her. "I'm thinking I'd like a commitment from you to go out more often than once. My lovely wife here likes to fish, but not way out on the Gulf waters. I understand you have a fishing boat. How about we work out some deep-sea buddy fishing trips for helping me get a good deal on the slip rental? And I'll raise you some river fishing time in exchange too."

"Please Paddy," Sophia said, raising prayer hands behind her puppy dog eyes. "I used to love fishing on the Wisconsin River back home. Scott takes me out on his pontoon now when I visit, but since you have this lovely river available here, I'd love to take advantage of it too."

"You drive a hard bargain, son, but you've got a deal! And tell you what, how about we all take my little boat upriver tonight to see our local fishing camp and get a bite to eat there?"

"Sounds like a good plan, sir," Jack said.

While Jack and Paddy went to the marina office, Scott suggested we pop in and see the inside of Gator's Seafood Market next door. "I've never been to one of these. I'm not sure what to expect."

"I haven't gone to one here, but I've seen some on the West Coast. So, it'll be new to me, too," I said.

The market was alive with its own unique energy. The sound of workers expertly moving and handling the various containers of seafood filled the air, along with a cacophony of chopping and slicing as they cut and cleaned the fish. The air was thick with humidity and the scent of saltwater and freshwater seafood. It was a combination of freshness and brine, a unique mix that can only come from seafood.

The seafood was displayed behind glass on refrigerated shelves as well as on the counters. From shrimp to river fish, it was an impressive sight to behold. Market workers were busy shucking oysters and preparing them for customers. The redfish were an orangey-pink, with beautiful, intricate patterns on their scales while the catfish were a deep gray. Scott was absorbed with watching as the market workers expertly filleted them.

"Jackie, come watch this," he called out. "No one in Wisconsin fillets as well as this."

The worker laughed. "If they did this day in and day out, they'd be experts too. Can I wrap some up for you?"

"No thank you. We're just tourists here," Jackie said. "May I take a photo of you and your work though?"

The man smiled and posed with a large catfish. "Please come back when you can try some of our seafood," he said before turning back to his work.

"This little town has such quaint vibes," Jackie said. "It feels more like a deep Southern or an eastern coastal town than other Florida cities I've visited."

"I know what you mean," Sophia said. "Tallahassee seems more a part of the deep south too with their live oaks instead of palm trees."

When Jack and Paddy returned to our group, we loaded the luggage in Maeve's golf cart for the ride up the hill to the Fulton Inn while the rest of our group walked.

"It's so nice to see you again, Paddy," Scott said as we arrived at the Inn. "You've really made a life for yourselves here. But I must admit I'm surprised you're taking on the remodeling and opening of an Irish pub. Pretty far removed from police work."

"That's been Paddy's dream ever since he left Ireland," Maeve said. "I couldn't say no to him. But now I'm thinking it may have been a poor decision. It is putting so much stress on him. And that is harder for us to handle as we get older."

"You're not that much older than us. Jackie and I are looking forward to retirement shortly. The process of handing off the day-to-day management of my construction business and the photography studio is in the works. We will be freed up to travel and enjoy our grandchildren with zero plans to open a new business."

"Sure, ya see, we never had a business. We look at this as more of a social club, like pubs in Ireland. We've found that the Southern attitude fits right in. Things move slower here, and people have no need to be rushin' about," Maeve said.

"That's what I feel here too. My own work is fast-paced and there is little time for shutting off my mind and my phone. All that immediacy of being able to reach someone right away can be exhausting," Jack said.

"Paddy, can we walk over and at least see the pub? Katie let us know about some construction issues. I'd be interested in hearing about them as it's my line of work," Scott said.

"Oh yes. We'd love to see the place," Sophia added.

Paddy shifted uncomfortably. "It's not a good time. There's been some further complications you haven't heard about. This is awkward to say, but…"

Just then a police car pulled up. The chief hopped out and walked up to us on the front verandah of the hotel. He tipped his hat and said, "Sorry to interrupt, but Paddy, can I have a word with you?"

"Sure, Chief." Paddy excused himself.

"Maeve, what did Paddy mean? What's delaying the opening?" Scott asked.

They should be told what happened and why the pub wasn't opening up as planned, but Maeve stalled. She looked toward me, so I answered Scott's question. "The darndest thing happened there last night. Seaside's mayor was in the building, unbeknownst to Paddy, and apparently took a tumble down the front staircase. He didn't survive it. The police wanted to take some time to investigate the incident in case there was foul play."

"Oh my goodness," Jackie exclaimed. "I'm so sorry to hear that. So, the typical yellow tape is on the doors and all that. Where is the pub located?"

"It's just a couple of blocks over," Maeve said. "We're hopeful that they will open it up soon. That's our Chief of Police. He and Paddy have become friends since they have shared experiences. Maybe that's why he stopped when he saw us here. To let Paddy know we can get back in now."

As the chief talked, Paddy's whole figure collapsed on itself with dejection. He stood looking down, hands stuffed in his pockets.

Awkwardly, our four guests excused themselves, saying they'd like to freshen up before we headed out to the River Lodge for dinner. I knew they sensed Paddy wasn't in an entertaining mood right now.

Maeve and I dreaded hearing what was said between the two men. The chief left, but before Paddy could compose himself, another man came walking up to him with a big grin on his face. The man clapped Paddy on the back and shook his hand. Whatever he had to say cheered Paddy up. Now that was a positive-looking encounter. Maybe it would brighten his mood.

I decided I'd make my exit also, telling Maeve I needed to pick something up at the drugstore and that I wanted to call my assistant in LA. "Hope the chief didn't have bad news for Paddy," I said as I hugged her and walked down the front steps to leave. Paddy nodded as I passed, giving me a weak smile.

CHAPTER TEN

Paddy's mood was greatly improved as soon as we set out on the river on our way to dinner at Shaw's River Lodge. I imagined Maeve helped with that. She was ever the optimist.

Sophia and Scott were excited to be on the Wimico River. For me, it was all new as well. The contrast from the coastal region we had just left behind was unbelievable. Now we were smoothly navigating the main body with smaller streams branching off. Every so often, small piers jutted out into the river, peeking out between the dense foliage on the banks. A few were new modern aluminum piers, but most were weathered gray wood. Fishing boats were tied on at some while others appeared abandoned, barnacles densely layering their wood pilings.

Sunset colors bled into the sky above the trees, which Paddy explained were live oaks, bald cypress, and tupelo. All was quiet except for the chirping of birds hidden away in the canopy of leaves and branches that reached out across the river's banks.

Paddy reveled in explaining how long the river was and how far inland it went, as well as its reputation as a haven for fishermen. He took pride in the knowledge he'd acquired about the Wimico River and its surrounding area.

Shaw's River Lodge was a one-story, low-slung building whose wood color matched the mossy trees and river around us. The exterior clearly showed where additions had been put on over the years, including lodging accommodations for the fishermen. It looked like the kind of place where you didn't have to keep up any sort of pretense about how great your life was. No pressure here. Except maybe regarding the size of the fish you caught.

Paddy turned off the boat's motor as we glided in. Lighting was low and the effect was like a movie set in some backwater. Perfect in dim shades of gray, with sunset colors above the mossy trees surrounding it. A few lights twinkled inside the lodge, and as we walked toward it, we began to pick up the sounds of voices and music playing.

Our group was warmly welcomed by a young woman in jeans and a T-shirt with the lodge's logo on it. She directed us to grab a table wherever we'd like. Paddy chose a table near the window, looking out toward the river.

Everyone seemed to know each other as they called out greetings with some teasing about the size of their catch today. The waitress told us that the special tonight was blackened redfish with saffron rice and collard greens.

Several people stopped by to say hello to Paddy. He let them know about the pub holding its opening on Saturday. The mayor's death didn't come up in conversation until one fellow appeared and clapped Paddy on the back. "Tough about old man Trimble dying in your place. Bet there's a roundtable of suspects, heh?"

The word suspects caught my attention. I turned my attention from Maeve and Jack discussing which local fish they wanted to try to listening carefully to what the man had to say.

"It might have been an accident," Paddy said weakly.

"Yeah right. Sure. You believe that? That why the yellow tape is flapping all around your place? Don't be a fool. The mayor managed to make a lot of enemies since he was voted in. Power corrupts. Even in a backwater town like ours."

Maeve looked up from her menu as the man's volume went up and my ears perked up too.

"If you know something, you should tell the chief." Paddy's words conveyed a hopeful tone.

But before the man could offer any more information, our waitress appeared and told the man he'd better watch what he said in the company of our guests. Could he be just a local big mouth, or maybe he'd had a few too many drinks?

"Nah, they all know the same things I do. Though there is one angle…" the man's voice trailed off as the waitress stepped up in front of him, her pen poised to take our order.

My attention shifted to the man walking in our direction. He could have been a model for Ralph Lauren outdoor sportswear, though his clothing was far from the designer's line. Instead, it was modest and practical. His softly waved hair was genuine, not the kind styled for a photo shoot. He held himself with confidence and exuded a casual charm lending itself to a very attractive first impression.

"Is this man bothering you nice folk?" he asked.

The man smirked. "Just discussing current events."

"Hi Jesse," Maeve said.

"Hey there, Maeve. Ready to open up?"

"No, not for a few more days. Did you hear the latest mess that got dumped in our lap?"

Jesse nodded. "That the mayor tumbled down your stairs? I did. Sorry to hear about that. He was a good customer. Liked to have a beer or two here, too. But why would that hold you up?"

"The chief wanted to gather evidence in case it wasn't an accident. We've had to change our opening to Saturday," Maeve answered.

"Seriously? That's too bad. He's a good cop. I'm sure he wanted to keep everything on the up and up. I can't wait to have you pour me a Guinness, Paddy," he said, discreetly stepping in front of the loud-mouthed man who slid away back to his bar stool with a scrawl on his face. "One of my favorite fishing trips was to the River Boyne."

"Fine fishing river that 'tis. I didn't know you traveled to fish. We'll have to talk more about that over our Guinness, which I'll be glad to pour you when that gaudy yellow tape gets taken down. Appreciate your support, Jesse."

Paddy proceeded to introduce everyone around the table. Telling Jesse that Jack had secured a spot at the

Seaside Cove Marina for his boat. Jesse politely greeted each of us but then got called away to take a phone call.

"Such a nice young man," Maeve said. "He's been very supportive of another pub coming to town. Just like Tyler out at the Rum Runner."

"I like the sound of that. Where is the Rum Runner?" Jack asked.

"Out on Horseshoe Island."

"Can we take the boat there?" Sophia asked.

"You could, but you'd have to moor on the cove side. The island is so narrow that you can easily walk across to the Gulf side where the bar is," Paddy added.

"We were just there Sunday night. Great place to watch the sunset from," I said. "And I experienced eating my first raw oyster there!"

Sophia smiled warmly. "We appreciate you encouraging us to check out Seaside Cove, I'm looking forward to moving the boat here. It's a shorter drive from Tallahassee and we might even be able to have a small second home here. But the biggest plus is having an in at Paddy's Pub," she said with a wink at Maeve.

"Just wait until you see our little Coffee Corner at the pub. You can walk over from the marina for that first morning cup. I'm going to be putting repeat customers' names on coffee mugs. I'll be sure to order two for you."

After our dinner, Paddy and I were the last of our group to leave when Jesse approached us. "Can I have a quick word with you, Paddy? Rumors are spreading about the mayor. Some of the guys who dock here are saying that he was in some sort of financial trouble too. Do you know anything about that?"

"Nope, hadn't heard that. But if they have some knowledge about it, please have them talk to the police. I'm afraid I've been shooting my mouth off about the delay, and now the chief thinks I might have enough anger in me to have pushed the mayor myself."

"Oh no. That makes it extra messy for you." Jesse turned to me and said, "I hope you'll come upriver again."

"It might be awhile. She's planning to return to Los Angeles," Paddy said.

"I'm sorry to hear that. Maybe you'll be back for a visit soon?"

"I know I'll be back. Seaside Cove is growing on me. I look forward to spending more time here in the future." That sounded so proper and grownup, but with him standing so close, I found myself almost tongue-tied. The reasons to visit more often were growing. Especially after hearing what Paddy just said. As soon as Jesse walked away, I asked. "Is that what the chief stopped to tell you? Why didn't you tell us that? He can't be serious."

"I have been talking too much and could have been overheard. Here I was starting to blame the delays on Mayor Marvin because of what others were putting in my ear. Darnell said he was told about it by more than one person. I would have never pushed him down the stairs or even raised a hand to him, but my words," Paddy let out a big sigh. "My words said something different."

Frustrated, I asked, "Who is this Darnell?" Was he another big talker like the guy we'd just heard, or a busy body in town?

"That's the chief's first name. We've become friends, and he even asked for my help in one or two of his tougher cases. But Katie, I can't blame him. It only shows me how seriously he's taking it."

"So, was I right? That's what he told you in front of the hotel earlier?"

"Right. Darnell said I should understand he can't share this case's details with me because I might be a suspect if it turns out to be murder. He asked me to come in for a talk. He called it talk, mind you. Can you believe that? I know he means an interview. I told him I'd come in anytime after today because of our visitors.

He was fine with that but tried to make a joke about me not leaving town. Please keep this to yourself for now... Maeve is under enough pressure."

In a quieter, less assured voice, he added, "This will blow over in a day or two."

CHAPTER ELEVEN

My surprise at what Paddy revealed at the lodge last night was with me as I woke up this morning. How could it be possible that he was being considered a suspect? I remembered the grumbling and impatience he displayed, but that hardly led him to purposely shove someone down a staircase. Was there something I missed?

Now I was sorry I'd promised to keep that information to myself, but Paddy told me that it would blow over, and he didn't want to burden Maeve or worry our visitors. I'll wait and see what comes today.

To take all our minds off the matter, we decided to spend the day out in Jack's boat on Wimico Bay. We wouldn't be doing any fishing, but this trip would offer a wonderful and welcome diversion for all of us. And with the added bonus of getting to see the bay and the islands from the water.

Maeve and Paddy were in the kitchen preparing a lunch basket for the day. We wouldn't be on a deep-sea fishing excursion this time, but that was okay.

* * *

The boat rode the small waves of Wimico Bay with ease. We passed under the causeway to Horseshoe Island, staying close to the shoreline for now. It was fun to see the town from this vantage point.

The fishing pier jutted out over the blue water, its sturdy beams supporting a variety of families and their fishing gear. Buckets filled with bait and nets stood at their feet as they cast their lines into the depths below. A young girl in a vibrant pink sunhat caught my eye and waved excitedly as we glided by. From this unique vantage point, I saw the town in a whole new light. With the slight incline, we had a clear view of the charming homes that hugged the shoreline. Maeve eagerly pointed out each one to Jackie and Sophia.

As we approached the pass we'd be taking to get out to the Gulf, Paddy explained the history of the uninhabited small barrier island to our right. "St. John Island is owned by the U.S. Department of the Interior as a protected wildlife refugee. Humans allowed only during the daytime. No high-rises or fast-food restaurants there."

We navigated through St. John Pass and soon found ourselves in the vast expanse of the Gulf. The sparkling water was dotted with small boats and sailboats, taking advantage of the beautiful day. From here, Horseshoe Island looked even more beautiful with its colorful stilt houses and white sandy beaches dotted with towels and umbrellas. Many more people were in the water today compared to the cooler night when we visited the Rum Runner.

At the far eastern end of Horseshoe Island, we saw the Wimico Inlet lighthouse. Maeve mentioned that Jack and Sophia might enjoy going to the museum there. "Oh and you must show up for our celebration of all things pirate in early summer. It's the most fun! There is a big parade in town with kids and pets dressed as pirates. And we'll help you decorate your boat for the boat parade if you like. There are dunking tanks that look like walking the plank. And guess how many gold coins are in a jar games. Course the coins are candy, so the kids like that one. Our neighbor Winnie had an amazing costume last year. She was a pirate queen."

"There are such things?" I asked. "I'll bet Winnie cut a dashing figure."

"Katie, you'd be perfect as the auburn-haired Grace O'Malley. She was a pirate queen from Ireland."

That set me thinking. How fun it would be to throw a party at the pub for that event. "Will you do anything special for the pirate celebration?"

Paddy shook his head. "Probably not. There is a lot going on for that already. But like Maeve said, it would be fun to be part of the boat parade with you, Jack. Suppose we could decorate up the pub a little bit."

"Can you text me the dates, Paddy? It sounds like a lot of fun," Sophia said. "I'm already picturing things we could do with the boat."

It was good to see Paddy relaxed and enjoying himself. And now I was tempted to make some suggestions for the pub to be part of the pirate party.

"Maybe you should think outside of the box, Paddy," Maeve said. "Owning a local business means we get to be a bigger part of the community. There has to be some way to add our input to the festival."

"Aye my sweet. But at the moment, I'm thinkin' we may have made a mistake in trying to make me lifelong dream come true and own a pub. With the money we've spent, I could have bought myself a grand boat and spent my days fishin'." And he clasped his hands behind his head, closed his eyes, and turned his face to the sun.

"Sure, you would've been bored out of yer mind,"

Maeve said. "And that dream would still been there niggling at you. You'll be grand with yer wee fishing boat and by having a mate with a seaworthy craft."

The two of them still cracked me up. What a pair.

"I find myself hoping I won't get bored with my retirement," Jackie said. "My work has taken me to your beautiful country several times. And each time, as soon as I've landed and gotten out into the countryside, there's a sense of calm and peace. I feel so welcomed. Especially at the pubs."

"Now aren't you sweet," Maeve said. "Then you are in the photography business like your parents? I knew them. Where have you traveled while you were on our Emerald Isle?"

"From Waterford to the Ring of Kerry to Dublin. Scott and I plan on traveling there soon too," Jackie said.

"I'm working on her golf game," Scott said. "We would like to play on the iconic courses of Ireland and Scotland."

"Sounds like you two youngin's will be kept busy. We thought we'd stay in Harmony after we retired, but the winter chill was getting mighty fierce on our old bones. We even toyed with going back to Ireland, which will always be home, no matter where we wander. But, when friends told us of the Gulf of Mexico shoreline, and we took a few trips here, felt right away like it just had to be! And when the old bank building came up for sale, and Paddy talked about buying it, I supported him."

"That building called out to me!" Paddy grinned contentedly. "We have no young ones of our own, though Maeve and I consider Katie family." He pulled me in tight for a hug. "Still, I hope all the folks who pass through Paddy's Pub feel they were welcomed to something special. If we ever open that tis."

Maeve pinched her lips. "There now. No more going down the poor me lane, mister. Sure, it's been a little harder than we thought, but we are this close to opening." She held her thumb and pointer finger close together and stuck them in Paddy's face, getting a big grin in return. "A year from now, we'll look back at this time and laugh that we ever got discouraged. And now we are on a boat with old and new friends on the beautiful blue water, so we are blessed."

After a light picnic lunch aboard the boat, we lazed about and soaked up the sun before heading back to the marina.

When Maeve suggested the Fulton Inn for dinner, Scott quickly shook his head. "We had breakfast there and were not all that impressed. If you don't mind, I'd like to go to the restaurant at Gator's. They have a nice view of the river and I'll bet the seafood is to die for."

"Fine by us," Paddy said. "You might enjoy walking

along the path in that area too. Get close-ups of all the different commercial fishing boats. Seaside Cove has a substantial fleet. In fact, the original Gator was a Greek who ran a small fleet of vessels to supply his fish market."

"Where did the nickname come from?" I asked.

"Story has it he battled a huge alligator and lost a foot in the process," Paddy said. "He's passed on, but his son Nicholas is the one who added the bar and grill at the back of the seafood market."

We pulled into Jack's rental slip at the marina and walked to Gator's Grill where the manager, Geno, greeted Paddy. "I've been expecting to have a shortage of oysters for our restaurant when you open the pub. With all your talk about the fresh oysters in your hometown of Clarinbridge, I figured I'd be having to outbid you to stock our place."

"Come Saturday, you will be," Paddy shot back at him with a hearty laugh.

"I'm sorry if the parking issue is making trouble for you, but it's been a problem for The Salty Dawg and Gator's ever since the town took out car parking along this side of River Road. I know most people here have golf carts, so I get that, but the council has to understand our problem, too."

"Yesterday they gave me a temporary parking waiver for Saturday. But to open the rooms upstairs I have to present my ideas for the possibility of some huge surge of cars needing parking spots. They've called a crisis meeting for this coming Monday night to get someone installed into the empty position of mayor, so I'm going to show them my plans then."

"Glad you mentioned it. See it's small-town stuff like that can be so irritating. I should let Butch from Salty Dawg know too in case he wants to attend. Now excuse me for appearing crass and may he rest in peace, but now that Marvin is gone, we might actually be able to work together with the council members and figure this out."

CHAPTER TWELVE

Very early Thursday morning, Paddy got a call from Slim, their chef at the pub. Paddy had been buttering his toast, so he put the phone on speaker. Slim explained he'd been there early for a food delivery and that the crime scene tape was down. "Good thing I took that gamble," Slim continued. "Now I won't have to get a police escort to accept the food delivery."

"I'll meet you there in a few minutes," Paddy said before hanging up. He took a hearty bite of his toast and grabbed his coffee travel mug. "Will you alert Hannah that it's a definite go for the grand opening on Saturday?"

"Well praise the Lord. Things are looking up," Maeve said. "I'll go with you to get the place ready."

"You two both go ahead. I have to catch up with

Kristen about a couple of things, but I'll be down shortly. And I'll stop in at Hannah's to let her know what's up," I said.

Maeve looked concerned. "Sorry if all this is hurting your business back in LA. We really appreciate the help you've been to us. I don't know how we would have done this without you, Katie. And don't be too long. Remember Sophia and Jack are coming back with Scott and Jackie to see the place before they leave today. I'm grabbing some muffins at the bakery for everyone." She was bubbly and full of excitement again now that they were guaranteed to open on Saturday.

During my Zoom call with Kristen, we wrapped up our business without me even being tempted to ask about Joel the Jerk. Big step on my end. I let her know that I would be staying in Seaside Cove a little while longer, briefly explaining that my uncle and aunt could really use my help. She seemed confident about handling things and welcomed being given more responsibility.

"Are you doing the planning for this grand opening event? Remember when we did that opening of that jewelry store in Beverly Hills? The security we had to hire! And then there was that new cafe on the board walk in Hermosa Beach with those street performers just outside. Anything like that happening with your uncle's place?"

"We've ended up with some good stories to tell! But nope, this will be much more low-key. I did hire two Irish musicians, which should kick it up a notch. Today I've got to get more fliers out, especially to the snowbird communities."

"You have snowbirds in Florida? Are they called that because they're all white?"

It took me a moment, but then I realized Kristen thought I was talking about actual birds, so I explained that these snowbirds are people who fly south during the winter, looking for warmer weather.

"So, you're in a town where much of the population is retired? Don't you miss the action of a bustling, exciting, cosmopolitan city like Los Angeles? What's that expression? Do they roll the sidewalks up after dark there?"

"Surprisingly I don't miss much," I said, realizing how very true that was. "I'll touch base with you in a day or two. Bye for now."

* * *

The horn toot I heard came from behind me. Winnie

stopped and rolled down her window. "Need a ride, kiddo?"

"Hey Winnie. No thanks. Decided to walk to the pub."

"How's it going there? Chief all done investigating? Or is there still a wild-eyed crazy murderer on the loose?"

"He's not arrested anyone yet. Great news this morning, though! Mark your calendar for Saturday's opening," I said. "Another day of food pickups for you?"

"Not today, darlin'. Today it's my turn to walk them sweet pups at the humane society. I reckon I'd best be getting on or they'll just do their business all over that kennel floor."

Before taking Main Street to the pub, I stopped in at the offices of the Cove Gazette. Hannah seemed genuinely surprised to hear the grand opening was going forward this weekend. Her reaction caught me off guard. She seemed hesitant to show pleasure in what I told her.

"Hannah, what is it? Something my aunt and uncle should know?"

"Katie, I received second-hand information that the chief is going to be interviewing your uncle about the mayor's murder."

How did she know that? Paddy thought he was

keeping it under wraps. I didn't want to confirm the truth of the rumors until Paddy was ready to do so himself.

"Well, that's not new. They talked extensively the past few days."

Hannah's eyes dropped down as she fidgeted with some papers on her desk. "There's been word flying around about how upset Paddy was getting about the delays and that he was laying the blame at the mayor's feet."

"Grumblings. From who? Is this still tied in with your theory about the pub being too much competition for the Bayview? I stopped there after we talked."

"You did? It's a nice place, isn't it?"

"It is, but they didn't seem very busy and there was a weird vibe there. Like a cloud over it."

Hannah nodded. "It's been slipping lately. And now, with the pub opening, it can only hurt them. Especially for parties and events. When the mayor realized that was going on, I'm sure he could see the writing on the wall."

"But why does that mean Paddy would want to hurt him? I'd think it would be the other way around."

"There's more to it than that. Did you know the cook your uncle hired used to work there? Some people think Paddy hired him away from Bayview. I personally think

Slim wanted out for a while. But the point is there were things happening that could have pushed Mayor Marvin to hurt Paddy's business. In his position as Mayor, I've found more than one person who's been impacted by a little power play from the mayor's office. He's the one who might have manipulated things and continually put up roadblocks with the needed permits to open."

"Sabotaging the opening? But what about the electrical issues, Hannah? So, the mayor tells the electrician to do wrong stuff? I can't believe that."

"Small towns have lots of connective tissue. You'd be surprised," Hannah said. "Now, change of subject. Are you coming to the book club with Maeve tonight?"

"I am. I didn't know you were a member."

"My family's writing expertise was in the journalism area. But I enjoy reading fiction and I want to keep on the good side of my mother-in-law."

"Is she the hostess of the club?"

"Yep. But all kidding aside, Eve's okay. I'll see you later tonight."

CHAPTER THIRTEEN

What a scene I walked into at Paddy's Pub!

The wait staff were being trained. A bartender was breaking in new trainees. And luscious smells of coffee and fresh baked goods wafted out of the Coffee Corner.

"Ah, my Katie girl," Paddy said, opening his arms as though to embrace the scene. "This is starting to feel real after weeks of being beaten down. Come on over here and meet another Irish cousin of yours. Liam Duffy, meet Katie Murphy. This fine Irish lass is a cousin of yours."

Liam and I both burst out laughing. He took off his tweed flat Irish cap and did a deep bow. "My pleasure. But Paddy, just how many Irish cousins do we all have?"

"I was thinking the same thing. We'll have to trace the lines back and see where they connect, but for now, it's good to know there's more family here," I said.

"When I heard about this place, I put a call in, and here I am. Much as I love my Irish home, this warm sunny weather tempted me away," Liam said.

Looking at the sweet face of Cousin Liam's and listening to his slight Irish accent, I could tell he was going to be a hot commodity in these parts.

Maeve came by and pinched his cheek. "Isn't he just the cutest? And he knows the ins and outs of Irish beers and liquors. We are lucky to have him." She called out to someone on the other side of the room. "No need to move that table. It'll work out just fine where it is. Excuse me, I'm needed elsewhere."

"Can I take a photograph of you behind the bar, Liam? It would be a perfect Facebook post and a good draw, especially for the young women in town," I said.

"Want me to do the four-leaf clover on top a glass of dark?" Liam asked. He reached for a glass and pulled the Guinness tap handle.

"I'll take that sample drink, barkeep," someone shouted. "And some for my friends, too."

It was Scott! Along with Jack, Sophia, and Jackie.

"We heard there was a party going on and we didn't want to miss it," Jack said.

"Welcome to Paddy's Pub," I said. "Before you get the

beer, I'll be taking a photograph of Liam's pour for advertising. He's the real thing, all the way from Ireland."

"When we saw that ugly yellow tape down, you know we had to stop in for a quick celebratory glass of Irish beer. Even though it's only ten in the morning here," Sophia said.

"But it's five o'clock somewhere!" Jack responded.

"Never truer words spoken." Paddy came walking out from the back hall, followed by a tall, deeply tanned man whose strong, weathered arms with gnarled lines and veins hung easily at his sides. His large hands were comfortably hooked into the pockets of his faded jeans. His face was deeply etched by age and elements. He was dressed simply in a clean, black T-shirt that hugged his muscular frame. His hair, a washed-out gray, was trimmed tightly against his head, accentuating his rugged features.

"Everyone, this is the best chef in all the panhandle. Slim O'Conner."

"Well don't know about that," Slim said, modestly dropping his eyes.

"Slim, I detect a slight Irish accent," Sophia said. Are you from Ireland too?"

"Yes, ma'am. But came here as a young lad and didn't think I had much of my Irish accent anymore."

"So, how did you end up working here?" Jack asked.

Slim opened his mouth but then looked toward Paddy before speaking, as though judging what he should say. "I've been head chef at another restaurant for years and just felt it was time to move on."

Slim's pause made me think he had picked his words carefully. Could he be the one Hannah mentioned leaving the Bayview? I couldn't believe Paddy would try to steal someone else's employees. No matter if he was the best chef in this area.

"Did that happen to be the restaurant at the Bayview?" Jackie asked. "If it was, I can say you are sorely missed."

Looking to quickly change the subject, Slim said, "I'm looking for some taste testers. Any volunteers?"

Everyone jovially agreed they'd do tasting duty and dishes were brought out for sampling. Rave reviews on the food were pouring in. Slim was beaming until I noticed him look up, a dark cloud crossing his face. I turned to see Chief Darnell had arrived. He stood by the entrance, quietly waiting, hat in hand. Paddy slowly walked toward him and led him away to the snug near the front window without anyone else really noticing.

The group continued their samplings from Slim, plus Liam added a few specialty drinks he was working on. Maeve approached me, asking where Paddy had gone. I pointed toward the snug where she could just see the edge of the chief's hat resting on the table. Her eyes widened with fright.

When they came out of the snug, Darnell, sensing our concern, lightened the mood by hooking his thumbs in his gun belt and saying, "It appears that you are serving alcoholic beverages in this establishment. Do you have a liquor license, Mr. Murphy?"

Now everyone held their breaths…

"Ah…it was delayed because of…" Paddy fumbled for words.

"Just kidding Paddy. I know it's on the way. If I wasn't on duty, I'd have one myself!"

Whew, he had me on the edge of my seat with that one. Maybe he'd given good news to Paddy. Had he found something in the investigation that pointed toward another suspect?

"Well, look who just arrived!" Paddy said, pointing toward the kitchen hallway. "The man of the moment! Our very own state inspector. Are we being given the go-ahead?"

"Yes, sir. I was just in back and cleared things. The coolers are operational after the electricity problems were solved. You are good to go. Serve all the food and drinks to the public that you want."

He handed a manila envelope to Paddy and cheers

rose all around as Paddy opened it and waved the permit around.

"I've got a frame waiting for this," Maeve said, grabbing the paper from him.

The officiant raised his finger and everyone quieted. "There is just one small thing to take care of as part of my final release."

Paddy's hands dropped to his side as his shoulders rounded down.

"I need to taste the products you will be serving. Starting with a Guinness!"

Laughter bounced off the walls. Liam gave a thumbs up and began to set up another one of the dark Guinness pints.

Yet another figure appeared at the entry. "I heard all the ruckus in here and thought it might be that you saw me coming with this!" He waved another manila envelope in the air. "Your temporary occupancy approved by the town council of Seaside Cove. And I'll have some of what he's having, and if there's a bit of that Shepherd's Pie left, I'd be happy to help take it off your hands. This is my last stop for the day and I skipped lunch."

The new vibe at Paddy's felt good. I took a moment to arrange a few of the photos I'd captured into a social media post and send it on its way. Jack, Sophia, Scott, and Jackie said their goodbyes. Jack assured us all that he had secured a slip in the marina here and looked forward to seeing everyone soon.

After they left, we all got back to work. Maeve sent me upstairs to check on how the event rooms looked since she was sure guests at the opening would want to see them. As I began to climb the staircase, I shivered. It was only a few days ago that a person had fallen down these steps. At the top, I glanced back down through the open ceiling entry and into the pub. What had Mayor Trimble been doing up here late on a Sunday night? Was anyone else here to witness or even cause his fall? Stop thinking about it, Katie, I scolded myself. It will sort itself out.

I was in the process of adjusting the position of an old settee in the Galway Room when Paddy came in. "That was one of the lovely pieces we found in the back storage room. Thank goodness the building remained heated and cooled so it didn't need any repair."

"Today went very well, didn't it? You have your permits for Saturday and things seem to be coming together. The chief seemed in high spirits. Did he have good news for you?"

"Not really. He wanted to pin down a specific time for my formal interview at the station tonight."

CHAPTER FOURTEEN

The mansion where our book club met was perched atop the highest point in Seaside Cove. As we approached the large wooden front door, I couldn't help but notice the knocker shaped like a ram. The houses lining the street were all of similar size, but none compared to the pristine condition of this particular one. I took a moment to admire the stunning view from this vantage point. From here, I could see the river, the causeway, and Horseshoe Island with its twinkling lights. And, of course, the remnants of sunset over the Gulf. It was a breathtaking sight.

"Ah, quite a view, isn't it?" Maeve exclaimed, reaching up to give the brass door knocker a good bang against the plate. "Wait until you see inside, lass. This is Eve's husband's family home. He's passed on now, God rest his soul. I understand he was one of Seaside Cove's finest citizens. And Eve, she knows everything and everyone in this wee town."

"Welcome, come on in." The woman who opened the door for us had a warm, welcoming smile. Gracious in the way only a certain generation of Southern women can be. Her unpretentious strand of pearls and discreet earrings were not ostentatious. As I was admiring her short, stylish haircut with its feathered gray streaks it hit me. But before I could say anything, she took my hand in both of hers. "Maeve's talked about her lovely niece. I'm delighted I finally got to meet you, Katie."

Thank you for including me, Mrs. Brooks." This woman hosting Maeve's book club was none other than the famous author E.L. Brooks herself.

"Please call me Eve. Now come on in and join the others."

"You have a lovely home. And such a terrific view of Seaside Cove."

She grinned. "Believe me, I know how very fortunate I am to live here with the natural beauty but also surrounded by the wonderful people of Seaside Cove. Then throw in that I get to kill for a living...I'm one lucky woman."

Maeve elbowed me. "That's her favorite line."

Eve walked ahead of us, turning to wink at me and

smile at Maeve. "I love to pull that one out every so often." She twisted her arm behind her back to give a palm up, and Maeve slapped it conspiratorially.

We were led to the home's library, a spacious room with high ceilings. The faint scent of old books and polished wood lingered in the air, mixed with the smell of fresh-cut flowers. There was so much to take in. Oriental rugs in deep, rich hues covered the hardwood floors. Against the far wall was a grand fireplace, its mantle adorned with family photos and porcelain sculptures. Above it hung a painting of what must have been the original owners of the mansion, their stern faces looking down at us. In front of the large windows sat a vintage mahogany desk with a well-worn leather desk chair. Numerous upholstered pieces were pulled into a circle where the other members of the book club sat.

After introductions were made all around, I let myself absorb the fact that I was sitting in the personal library of one of my favorite authors. Everyone talked in low voices until Eve called the book club group to order by gently tapping her wine glass with the edge of her diamond ring.

"First, I want you all to know that I spoke to our absent member Vivian Trimble, offering her the club's condolences. I also sent her a bouquet of flowers from our group. I want to let you all know that with the help and support of family and friends, Vivian is doing well after such a devastating event. She was very appreciative and informed me that funeral arrangements had been made. I believe the obituary has already been published?"

Hannah nodded. "Yes. Because of the delay for the autopsy, the family has scheduled a wake and visitation at the Green Funeral Home for Monday. It will be running all day and into the evening. Then the funeral service and burial will be on Tuesday."

"Autopsy? Why? I thought it was a dreadful fall. Did they say what happened?" Peaches asked. "I've been out-of-town visiting with my dear sister in Tallahassee, so just found out about this situation yesterday."

"Oh right. How is she doing?" Loretta asked. "You mentioned she'd fallen and broke her hip. That friend of mine, I've told you about her, haven't I? The one living over in Pensacola. She never got over her broken hip surgery. Never really recovered after they went in and pinned it."

"She's okay. On the mend," Peaches responded. "Her daughter was a dear and of so much help. Her husband is not very understanding, I'm afraid, and was slow to respond to her personal needs. You know how that goes. I'm just grateful her children stepped up."

Marge cleared her throat and spoke up. "But back to Marvin. What happened?"

All eyes were on Maeve as she took over. Choosing her words carefully, she explained that it was a shock to her and Paddy. "We have yet to know the reason he was even in the pub at that hour. And certainly don't know what happened to cause him to fall down the staircase."

"Who would push that dear elderly man? And in your restaurant," Peaches exclaimed.

"Now Peaches, Maeve just said they didn't know what caused the fall," Marge scolded.

Maeve was unsure just what to say. She had to be hoping it was an accident. Paddy was having the interview, or should it be called interrogation, with the chief tonight. I planned on telling him that I couldn't keep this from Maeve any longer. That she shouldn't be kept in the dark, no matter how loving the intent.

Eve asked, "Was there any evidence of a struggle at the top of the stairs? Maybe he'd interrupted a burglar. Both my friendship with Vivian and my novelist mind are inquiring."

Hannah took over describing what was known so far as far as her paper had reported. "They've been combing the site for evidence and removed the police tape today. The chief already has told Vivian that this was being investigated as a murder because it appears he was struck on the back of the head with a blunt object prior to his fall. He's concluding that the strike caused him to fall and tumble down the stairs."

That was news to me! I was surprised by that. Paddy didn't mention it. Had the chief told him that earlier today? Was he keeping more from me? Trying to protect both me and Maeve?

Maeve's eyes widened. "Oh, I didn't know that."

Peaches snorted. "The way I've seen Marvin stumbling around after a night on the town, he does not need but a tiny pointer finger touch and he would have tumbled down."

"Peaches! That's uncalled for." Loretta snapped back. "The poor man is dead. Show him a modicum of respect."

"Sorry, but it is also true," Peaches protested. "Watch Vivian herself. Once she's soaked up all the sympathy, she'll be singing a different tune."

Marge asked. "Which staircase was his body found by? If it had been the back staircase, there is that ghost story about the former banker's wife. I think anyone who's seen Mrs. McCracken's ghostly figure, it was around the back area of the building."

"The body was at the bottom of the front staircase," Hannah said. "Have you seen the ghost yet, Maeve?"

"Ghost? Goodness no! But certainly, our capable

police department will figure out what happened. We'd better get going on our book discussion or my niece will doubt that we're a serious group," Maeve said, desperately trying to get away from the conversation about the mayor's death.

I'd never been part of a book club, but it appeared it was an enjoyable experience for them all. This group took their discussion seriously. Since I hadn't read their book of the month, I added very little to it but was fascinated to listen.

They stayed on the book topic, that is, until they were discussing a particular plot line involving the power play...the tug and pull...between the grandmother and her new husband over the treatment of her illegitimate grandchild.

"Speaking of power, who is stepping into the mayor's spot now?" Loretta asked.

That question broke up the group's focus. Ideas were tossed out for possible candidates.

"Do you think Vivian or her brother will toss their hat into the ring?" Maeve asked. "They would know what it entailed."

Eve pondered it for a moment before saying, "Not a bad idea. The Fagan family has always been involved in local politics and strong advocates for Seaside."

"Maeve, I've been wondering if you and Paddy

opening a new place might have been worrying for the Trimbles because it would be direct competition for the Bayview. I think we can all agree that the inn and the restaurant have really gone downhill over the past years," Loretta said.

"I hadn't thought of that, to be honest," Maeve said. "We always felt that we'd be welcomed. Tyler out at Rum Runner is putting our grand opening posters up at this place. And Marge, your son Jesse has been very helpful to us as well."

Hmm…so Marge is Jesse's mother? Maeve had only told me she ran the shop in town where Maeve's sewing circle met. But I should have expected to meet more family connections as my circle of acquaintances grew.

"I heard Paddy stole the Bayview's head chef. Certainly, that would cause bad feelings," Peaches said.

"That's not true," Maeve protested. "Slim applied for the job with us." I could tell that Maeve was more than ready to leave, and she nodded eagerly when I said we'd better head home.

As we were leaving, Hannah called for her husband to join us so he could meet me. I didn't realize they lived here with Eve. While we waited, she explained that Greg helped his mother work on her books.

"He's an expert on forensics and procedural techniques and technicalities. Eve plots rough drafts and

Greg flushes them out with specifics. One day he may co-write with her too," Hannah added.

Greg came down the curved staircase and introduced himself. "I love my mother and her sweet Southern way, but don't let that fool you. She writes bloody crime thrillers. So, her genre provides me with lots of opportunities for research."

"Like all the ways to poison someone, or how to pull fingerprints off decades-old paper," Hannah added.

"Are you tasked with keeping the dynasty going?" I asked.

Greg laughed. "I guess you could say that, but Mom has a long writing life ahead of her, so I'm just pleased to share in her glory. I hope you enjoyed the book club meeting. You all do actually read books, don't you? I can always hear the chatter and laughter from my office upstairs so I wonder if this is a serious sort of club."

"We do. And tonight, there was a lot of talk about our own local murder," Hannah said.

"Hmm, yes. I suppose it will consume the town for a while. Quite the story in here."

CHAPTER FIFTEEN

On the walk home, I told Maeve how much I enjoyed meeting Eve. "And you didn't tell me she was E.L. Brooks! One of my favorite authors," I said.

But Maeve seemed distracted. Something other than the book club was on her mind. "I wonder if Paddy knows about the autopsy conclusions. It certainly changes things. Paddy is friends with the chief, so he must know about this. Maybe that's what Darnell told him today when he stopped in at the pub. I'm feeling so overwhelmed. Like things are spinning out of control."

We were almost home, and I decided to pull her mind in a different direction. I asked, "What was that ghost story Marge was talking about?"

Shaking her head, Maeve said, "Never heard about it before."

Paddy pulled up in his very quiet electric golf cart, startling both of us. "Ghost story?"

"Don't sneak up on us like that!" Maeve scolded. "Just some chatter about a former bank president's wife. They said she haunts the bank building."

"If true, it would enhance your Halloween party," I said. "I'll have to ask the mortuary family what they know about it. Maybe they saw her when they lived in the building."

"It's nice of you to give us ideas Katie, but I think we'll have our hands full running the pub. Besides, much as I want to believe my ideas about parking will work, the issue is still out there. I've offered options like special event shuttles from another parking lot for bigger events. And I think I can get agreements to rent parking lot spaces from adjoining businesses."

"Let's assume you clear the parking hurdle," I answered. "You've got those rooms upstairs. The Waterford with that beautiful fireplace and the big windows facing the street, and the Limerick with large wood paneled sliding doors that connected it with the Kilkenny to create an even larger space. I love the Cork room with the elaborate crown molding and detailed chair rail. I'll bet there's not another place in a hundred miles with the appeal of the spaces on the second floor."

"We'll see how it goes. I'm hoping a big one will be St. Patrick's Day in March," Paddy said.

"Maeve talked about the pirate-themed celebration in June. I think you should embrace the uniqueness of the local events. And have brunches for the big holidays like Thanksgiving and Easter. Lots of the people here don't have family in the area or are retired, and I'm sure they'd love to have a common welcoming place to go out for those holidays."

"Okay, we get the message, Katie. Sounds like we could use a party planner! Do you know of a good one?" he said.

"I only wish I could be in two places at once." I said goodnight and kissed each of them on the cheek.

As I stepped into the house to go to bed, I heard Maeve ask, "Paddy, did you know that the mayor was hit on the back of the head before he fell down the stairs?"

"I heard about it," Paddy said. "Darnell told me today."

"Why didn't you tell me? Does he have any suspects?"

Silence. I held my breath. Would he tell her the truth now?

"Yes, he does."

"Who?"

"Me."

A loud gasp from Maeve…then a low, long moan.

"I'm afraid so," Paddy said. "I wanted to tell you sooner, but I thought it would just all go away. At first, I hoped they would rule it a horrible accident. Now that the examiner revealed the blow to the back of his head, surely there will be more clues to find. Or someone would have heard or seen something."

"How long were you going to keep this from me?" she asked.

"I'm so sorry. I should have told you sooner. I didn't want you to worry, and like I said, I thought it would all go away. But Darnell interviewed me tonight. Officially. He'll be reaching out to you regarding this, but I know you were sleeping."

"Paddy, why does he even think it could be you?"

"I'm afraid I got to flapping my lips too much during this whole process. Could have been the building inspector or one of the plumbing people overhearing things. In fact, one of the electricians told me that someone in the chain of command is messing with me. He said I should watch my back in this small town. There are big egos around, and I'm still new here."

"So that's why the suddenly glum face when we headed out to the island on Sunday. It was that Rooster guy, wasn't it?" Maeve asked, her voice rising with concern. "Did you tell the chief about that?"

"Not yet. It seemed like just gossip. I mean, he didn't

name anyone. But maybe I should ask Rooster what he meant. Maybe he has proof of some kind. It's just not in my makeup to push people," Paddy said hesitantly.

"You're darn right to ask what he meant! Especially since the focus seems to be on you now. Were they still at the pub working when we dropped you back to get your golf car?" Maeve was not going to let this slide.

"Yes, and Tim Douglas was there, too."

"And then you came home?"

"Right." Paddy sounded exhausted. "We should turn in Maeve. We have a lot of work to do tomorrow."

But she remained tenacious. "And you didn't go back out?"

Silence. Paddy didn't answer her, but I heard them both entering the house.

I slid further into the shadows in the living room, breathlessly waiting to hear his answer, but afraid to be discovered eavesdropping.

"Patrick?"

Silence.

Footsteps in my direction.

"Answer me now. And tell me the truth."

"You know, don't you?" he said in a low voice.

CHAPTER SIXTEEN

I spent a restless night trying to piece things together. When I went into the kitchen for my morning coffee, Maeve was already up. She probably didn't sleep much either. A dark cloud hung over the grand opening coming up.

In silence we took our coffee out to the front porch. The morning quiet was broken by Winnie coming over from her yard.

"Is your company gone?"

"They are. They boated away yesterday," I said.

"Too bad about the mayor. Have they arrested anyone yet?"

I shook my head. "Nope."

"But I saw that your grand opening will be Saturday. And that's a good thing."

"Would you like a coffee, Winnie?" Maeve asked in a quiet tone.

"Nah, I'll be taking off soon. If it's Friday, it's Winnie's beauty shop day."

"So, a nice relaxing day getting your hair done?" I asked.

I heard a low chortle from Maeve. At least that broke her glum mood.

Winnie gave her thigh a hearty slap. "Darn, but that's a funny one." She ruffled and poofed up her hair. "Does this look like it's seen the inside of a hair salon in a month of Sundays? Heck no, I cut and style my own hair. But come Fridays, I become a manicurist for those sweet ladies in the nursing home. They just love having their nails painted up. Makes them feel right special. And we talk, oh my, do we talk! It's just some good old-fashioned fussing over them that I do."

"That is so sweet," I said. "You are a very generous woman, Winnie."

"I got the time is all. When I was at the Humane Society on Wednesday, I told them they should come on to your opening and check Paddy's Pub out. Maybe they could use your place to do one of their fundraisers. They're always running fundraisers. People love them animals."

"Wow excellent idea!" I turned to Maeve. "See how easy it would be to market your place as an event place."

"It sounds good, but like Paddy said, it might be too much for us to handle. Paddy is satisfied with just an Irish pub, not something bigger."

"Now listen here, Maeve, you're in the panhandle of Florida, not your hometown of Clarinbridge. I'll bet your square footage is about ten times what those ole pubs back in Ireland are. So, either Paddy rents out the other spaces and just keeps a corner of the building for a small pub, or you can offer up some mighty fine spaces to hold fancy events at," Winnie said.

"She's right, you know. A dream is one thing, but Paddy's bitten off an awfully big chunk of a building to chew without generating more income to cover expenses," I said.

"And I told you I'd keep my ears open, didn't I? Well, I heard some conversation. Might mean something. Might not. But in my mind, it fits together right snug with other stuff goin' round. Like how bad the Bayview is doing. A gal at the shelter thought it was so sweet that they found the mayor's dog, Tootsie, lying by the mayor's body. Now I'm not one to go 'round spreading rumors, so you better listen close the first time. We have a groomer who comes to clip dogs' nails. She said she had an emergency call from Vivian Trimble that Tootsie needed a trim. She wanted Tootsie to make a good show at the funeral. That's what Vivian is all about. Appearances."

"But what does that have to do with the murder of Marvin?" I asked.

"Wait. There's more. The groomer said she'd have to charge extra because it was a rush job and she was totally booked. Well Vivian gave her a piece of her mind. And she didn't appreciate it, especially cause she always wants a deal. What I took away from it was that either Vivian's cheap or she's running out of all that family money the Fagans had."

Winnie paused, waiting for a response. "Well, isn't that news?

"I'm not sure. So, are you saying maybe the mayor was killed by someone he owes money to?" Maeve said.

"Something like that. It's a piece to throw into the puzzle. I don't have occasion to socialize with the Trimbles, but they sure do want folk around here to make them think they are a step up on the social and economic ladder."

Neither Maeve nor I replied.

"Everyone okay this morning?" Winnie asked. "I swear I'm seeing the longest faces west of the river. Opening canceled again?"

"Oh no, it's set for Saturday," Maeve said. "If my husband's not in jail."

"What'd he do?" Winnie asked.

"Should I tell her?" I looked toward Maeve.

Winnie gracefully lowered her large, imposing frame onto the wicker chair. Her movements were confident and unwavering as if she had no doubts about the sturdiness of the furniture. The chair creaked slightly under her weight. "What's that mean? What's he suspected of?"

I explained how this all came up, including Chief Darnell's getting the autopsy that showed that an injury on the back of the head happened before the fall. "Paddy wanted to save Maeve from worrying. But she put two and two together after the book club meeting last night."

Winnie's brow furrowed as she looked at me. "He told you though, didn't he girl? You knew ahead of time."

"Katie, you knew? How could you not tell me?" Maeve cried.

"He admonished me not to tell you. I felt so bad about it. I was going to talk with him and tell him I could no longer keep quiet. But when you figured it out last night, well, I didn't have to."

"You shouldn't feel bad, girl. He should feel bad. That old coot telling you, a young city girl and not his own wife. Maeve is one strong lady, and Paddy better get it through his head that she deserves more respect than that. Hearing that her husband is a suspected murderer at the Brooks' house, for god's sake. That author lady kills people all the time, but this is real-life stuff right here."

"Real death stuff, you mean," Maeve said. "And don't yell at Katie. Honestly, I'm disappointed in Paddy not telling me, but if he has Katie as a sounding board, I'm okay with that." She turned her tired eyes toward me. "But I am sorry he burdened you with the knowledge. Staying with your old aunt and uncle sure isn't turning out like you thought it would, eh?"

CHAPTER SEVENTEEN

Maeve didn't bring up the discussion I'd eavesdropped on last night. What did Paddy think she knew? It was something between them and none of my business. But I naturally tended toward problem-solving, and it was hard not to think about the possibilities here. In my heart, I couldn't imagine Paddy having anything to do with hurting the mayor, but the way Maeve had questioned him about Sunday night left me wondering. But for now, I would keep looking forward and pray things would sort themselves out soon.

Now I would focus my attention on social media and helping to get things ready for the grand opening of Paddy's Pub tomorrow. I'd already notified the Sheehan duo and Hannah regarding the final date for it. Checking the pub's Facebook page, I was pleased to see we had over five hundred followers already. And a few creeps who implied the place was jinxed because someone died there. Did they mean the mayor or the ghost lady? Not nice, but soon enough, the murderer would be found and this would all blow over.

* * *

Every hand was on deck at the pub today. Glassware was being polished and napkins were wrapped around silverware. There would be a limited menu tomorrow if guests wanted a sit-down dinner, but Paddy and Maeve figured most people would just want to check the place out and see what remodeling had been done. They would enjoy the free small plate offerings and of course a pint or two.

I was delighted that Eve showed up late Friday afternoon, saying she was just out and about and thought she'd pop in. "Congratulations! I'm sure you'll bring only good things to our town. This is just stunning. The transformation from a mortuary to an Irish pub is astonishing."

Paddy grinned. "That's kind of you. I hope what happened here Sunday won't remind people of what this place had been."

"There might be a few curious folk, but give it a few weeks, and no one will even think about it."

"From your lips to God's ears," Maeve said.

"Now that I see the place, I know that I'd like to book a party. My next book will be published in about a year. It involves a drug cartel and drug running on the Gulf Coast, so this would be the perfect launch party spot! Get some of those big city publishers and agents down here to see how beautiful the coast is."

Maeve excitedly clapped her hands. "Perfect. Our first booking. Come with me to give me some more information and what date I should pencil in. Isn't that exciting, Paddy? A party already on the books."

"She's just being nice," Paddy said to me as he watched Eve and Maeve walk away.

"No. This isn't some little kid's birthday party," I said. "I've done launch parties in LA, and believe me, it's a big deal when it's a book from an author as well-known and successful as E.L. Brooks."

Paddy shrugged. "Really? Guess I'm out of that loop. Maeve said you enjoyed the book club last night. I imagine they had some gossip about the murder and all."

"Sure they did. Of course, people are talking about it. And expect curiosity seekers tomorrow. But given time, I'm sure the chief and his staff will figure out what happened. There is one thing from this morning that you might want to mention to him. According to the Trimble's dog groomer, the Trimbles are running low on funds."

"From a dog groomer? I don't know. So much of this sounds like everyone is jumping on the I-know-something train. Trying to one-up each other."

"But maybe, just maybe, if those thin threads are followed, pulled, unraveled, the true culprit will be revealed."

"You could be right. Why doesn't the groomer go to the chief herself?"

"Good question. But instead of waiting for that to occur, at least bring it up with him. You are friends. Remember that."

Paddy carefully considered what I said. "Katie, I know he's my friend, but I think bringing second and third-hand information and opinions to him will only look desperate on my part."

Our conversation was interrupted when Maeve came back asking if I'd show Eve around. "She's in the old bank vault. I'm heading back into the kitchen. We're training a new hire on plating meals, and I want to make sure the final presentation looks as I'd envisioned it."

The vault door, marked with its maker's stamp, was wide open, and Eve stood inside the compact eighty-square-foot space. The brass-faced lock box drawers were still intact, firmly fixed to the wall. A sturdy wooden table remained in the middle of the room.

"I've been told you can't get locked in, that the mechanism has been modified. But I wouldn't try it," I said.

Eve laughed. "You read my mind. I used a bank vault once in a story and did some research for that. That was before Greg was around to help. Does Paddy have plans for this, or will it remain a novelty?"

"I'm not sure what will be done with it."

"It makes me think of wine or bourbon tasting rooms for some reason. Oh well, I'm glad you agreed to give me a tour. I hope it's not a bother," Eve said. "I understand you have an event planning business in Los Angeles. That must be very interesting. You are probably able to help the Murphys with some ideas for this pub."

"Hopefully. I'm especially excited about the banquet rooms being available. I'm not sure what you envision for your launch party, but would you like to see the rooms upstairs?"

"For sure," Eve said. "I'm open to how it can be done."

"Would you like to take the stairs or the elevator?"

"If I remember correctly, there are two sets of stairs in this building. My husband's family was on the board, so I'm familiar with behind-the-scenes space." Eve carefully looked around before leaning closer. In a low voice, she said, "I'd like to use the staircase that the mayor tumbled down."

Well now, that caught me by surprise, but I accommodated her by walking back up toward the front of the building where the staircase was. Was she really interested in a book launch or here for writing material?

Eve took my arm and moved me against the hall wall so we wouldn't be overheard. "Katie, I can sense what you're thinking. I want you to know that my book launch party wasn't just a ruse. It's genuine, and I want it to be held here. My author mind kicked into gear after our book club meeting last night. I'm sure you wouldn't be surprised to learn that we authors often draw inspiration from real crimes to create our novels. I couldn't resist the temptation of delving into this real-life tragedy happening in our own backyard. I think you have a keen eye for detail and know more than you let on. You are in a unique position. Please indulge me. I know I murder people and can manipulate the clues and suspects as I wish, but maybe the experience I've acquired solving crimes in my books could translate into helping solve a real-life crime."

Her words were intriguing. She had a point. Could she draw on her knowledge built from the crime and mystery thrillers she'd written? "I'll indulge you on one condition. That you keep me in the loop if you have any lightbulb moments. My uncle is on the suspect list, and though I know he didn't do it, the easiest way to get this cleared up is to find who did."

"And it would be best if we find concrete proof or get a confession," Eve added as she gave me a fist bump. "Now onward and upward. If we can keep this to ourselves for now, I'd appreciate it. It might come to nothing. I wouldn't want to raise anyone's expectations."

We? Am I working with E.L. Brooks to solve a murder? Act cool about it, Katie, I admonished myself. "Mayor Trimble was found at the bottom of the staircase we are about to go up. He lay sprawled on his back with his dog Tootsie lying next to him."

Eve's eyes popped wide open. "The dog died too?"

"Oh no. Sorry. That didn't come out right. The dog stayed with him during the night. She's fine. Actually, I have something to share about the dog that I overheard this morning."

When we got to the second floor, Eve stopped to take in the view down to the hardwood floor at the landing. She carefully walked along the short stretch of hallway that had a railing on it looking into the entry hall below. Then she walked back and looked carefully at the banister, the floorboards, and the hall carpet runners.

"Katie, you arrived shortly after he was found?" Eve asked. "Correct?"

"Yes, the chief called my Uncle Paddy to come down to the pub because of what his chef Slim discovered. Let me explain. Slim was here very early to open the kitchen for a delivery. Then this little dog came walking up to him. He figured the dog had gotten in somehow and made himself at home for the night. Slim called the phone number on the dog's tag, and he heard the phone ringing somewhere inside the pub. That's when he found the body and called the police and Paddy."

"Slim? Wasn't he the chef at the Fulton Inn?"

"Yes, he was. Maeve was discombobulated…being woken up at five AM will do that to you. She asked me to follow Paddy over here, even though she didn't know specifically why he was called."

Eve walked toward the Donegal room and carefully looked around. "Anything about the object that was used to strike him?"

"Not that I've heard. Why aren't you calling it a murder weapon?"

"Can't. Not yet. I don't believe the police know if he died from the blow to his head or the fall down the stairs. Did you see any blood on the body that morning?"

"I didn't, but then I was kept back from the body."

"Who was there when you arrived? Besides police."

"Mrs. Trimble was there with her brother. Everyone

else seemed to be there in a professional capacity. Oh, but Hannah was there too. And Slim, of course."

We walked into the Waterford room, and Eve carefully surveyed her surroundings. "Pretty space," she remarked, admiring the fireplace. Her eyes continued to scan the room as she moved toward the windows and admired the view. "One of my books involved what appeared to be an accidental fall down a staircase."

"And I'll bet it turned out to be a murder," I said realizing what she was hinting at.

Her eyes turned toward me. "Yes, it did."

CHAPTER EIGHTEEN

Finally, the day of the official opening of Paddy's Pub was here!

The bar, imported all the way from Ireland, was a sight to behold with its gleaming brass foot rails and polished wood. Sunlight streamed through the stained-glass windows and transoms, creating dazzling rainbows inside the rooms. Vases held showy green Bells of Ireland mixed with yellow zinnias.

The staff was ready and looking great. The men wore white shirts with green armbands and sported shamrock-covered suspenders to hold up their black trousers. While the women dressed in playful white blouses with puffed sleeves trimmed in green, paired with either black skirts or pants. I volunteered to dress up too in case help was needed. The outfit felt a little odd at first, but it put me in an entertaining frame of mind.

Everyone was energized and eager to open the doors. Liam and two other bartenders stood ready to take orders. The Sheehan duo was set up. The wait staff was ready to go with trays of samples for the guests to try.

When the doors opened, there was a line outside waiting to get in. Paddy and Maeve stood at the door, ready to greet everyone.

Some guests turned first to the right to check out the coffee and gift shop area. Maeve's eclectic assortment of wooden tables and chairs, found at garage sales, estate sales, or flea markets, created a relaxed, quiet corner with a serving counter for basic coffees and teas, along with fresh baked goods from the kitchen. A display of local quilt wall hangings from the Sew-Sew Shop was tucked in one corner. Local artists' works were displayed on the walls. Cubbies, with coming soon signs, displayed photographs of T-shirts, caps and other promotional products I'd convinced Paddy to order.

Those who turned left would find themselves in the main pub and dining area. Despite its capacity for many customers, the space was designed to feel cozy and intimate. I could easily envision Paddy and his friends gathered around playing pinochle by the fireplace in the corner. In another corner, there was a small settee and side chairs with stained glass lamps. Even at the larger bar, there was still a sense of closeness and warmth that was sure to make people feel welcome.

Hannah appeared next to me and pointed to Paddy. "Campaigning to run for Mayor himself?"

"Hah, I doubt it. He'll have his hands full here," I responded. "Being Mayor of Seaside Cove is the last thing on Paddy's mind."

"Well, I am one of many who are glad to see this opening finally happen."

"Me too!"

"Now if Paddy can just get out from under the murder investigation," she said.

"Hush. We will not speak of that today." I laughed, making an X with my fingers.

The loud screech of microphone feedback caused everyone to turn their heads toward Paddy, who stood on the small stage, ready to make a speech.

"I'd like to extend a warm welcome to each and every one of you and thank you for coming today. Maeve and I know most of you already, but we're excited to get to know the rest of you. Opening a pub, or a public house as we call it, has been a lifelong dream of mine. As some of you may have seen on our social media pages, I hail from Clarinbridge, famous for its delectable oysters. So, settlin' here just felt right."

A low chuckle rippled through the gathered crowd.

"Me dear wife is from Kenmare. We named our new home here after it, as it has two meanings…little nest and head of the sea. Both seem quite fitting for our situation, don't ye think? But where was I going with this?"

The crowd erupted into laughter.

"I see you know what I'm talking about!"

Chants of *have another pint Paddy* filled the air.

"And I'll be doin' just that soon enough. But before I go off celebrating, I wanted to say that seeing all you fine folk here today proves that we made the right decision in settling down in this lovely town."

Paddy reached for the Guinness someone in the crowd handed up to him. His face was filled with emotion. And with a crisp bop of his head and raise of the pint, he said, "Sláinte!"

Shouts of *cheers* went up across the room.

Paddy wasn't aware that Maeve had snuck up behind him until she tapped his shoulder. "Hold on old man, I've something for you." Two of the wait staff came out carrying framed prints. With puzzled eyes, Paddy reached in to pull out his reading glasses and peer closely at the black and white prints.

"Well, praise be. It's meself at the old pub in Clarinbridge. Woman, you are amazing." And in a bold move, he hugged Maeve and dipped her back, landing a big kiss on her lips.

Watching my aunt and uncle and knowing all they'd gone through to get to this point, I thought it safe to say everyone agrees it was NOT a poor decision to put an Irish Pub here on the Florida Panhandle!

Tables were pushed aside for the dancers from Pensacola to begin performing, with the Sheehans providing musical accompaniment. Following a series of lively, high-stepping dances and jigs, the dancers kindly offered to share their techniques with others.

Winnie was the first person to take them up on the offer. She was surprisingly light on her feet despite the extra pounds she carried. Maeve soon joined her. It was obvious she'd done this before. Three giggling teens were convinced to give it a go, too. The crowd clapped along in rhythm with the music.

As I walked through the pub, keeping an eye out for anything that needed tending to, I was delighted to be asked about bookings for parties. My promotions on social media were proving positive.

Tyler Berman waved at me from across the room and gave me a big thumbs-up. It was the person standing next to him that made me shriek and run over.

"Kristen! What a surprise! What are you doing here?"

"Hey, slow down," she said. "It's all good. I just wanted to surprise you. And this gorgeous and very friendly man helped me out."

"Tyler? You did? How?"

"Good old internet," Kristen said. "I saw the photos you posted of the dinner with Paddy and Maeve on the beach. In some of them, the Rum Runner sign showed. I remembered you telling me what a good time you had there and about the nice guy who owned the place. So easy enough to put this surprise together. Tyler picked me up at the airport this morning and here I am."

"So, you think I'm a nice guy?" Tyler teased. "I'll take that as a positive."

"I did, and now I know for sure. Thanks so much for helping her out. That was super sweet of you. Come on, I'll introduce you to Paddy and Maeve. Okay with you, Tyler?"

"Sure, you go ahead. I'm going to grab some of those appetizers I've seen floating on by."

CHAPTER NINETEEN

The opening last night made the front page of the Cove Gazette and the pub was already busy when I arrived for Sunday brunch with Kristen. Hannah was a doll to get her article about the opening posted so quickly. We ordered the traditional Irish breakfast of sausages, baked beans, eggs, mushrooms, grilled tomatoes, and a potato hash. A plate containing toast, butter, and marmalade was set before us, along with our coffees.

Last night, Kristen and I talked about life and love. She'd told me that she was engaged to her longtime boyfriend, and they planned a wedding on the beach. She asked if I wanted to talk about Joel, my ex-employee and ex-boyfriend.

A wave of emotions hit me all at once. I had been trying so hard to suppress them, but seeing Kristen again brought it all rushing to the surface. She knew Joel Carter from our time working together at my company. Kristen was not just an important employee but also a close friend. I turned to her for support when Joel broke up with me through a casual text. Who does that?

Joel's ambition was to climb the political ladder in California, and that meant having the right partner by his side. At one of my parties for a local alderman, funded by his wealthy supporter, Joel saw an opportunity. The financier took a liking to him and got him a position as an aide for the alderman. Joel eagerly accepted, as it would set him on a path in political circles. It just happened that the financier had a beautiful daughter who was popular on social media. That's where I first caught wind of Joel's deceitful actions of spending time with this girl and her friends while lying to me about it. I suppose being a redhead Irish girl didn't fit into his plans of ingratiating himself into California's political elite. He thought the blonde Valley girl, Suri, was a better match for him. So good riddance.

We had a heart-to-heart last night, but since Kristen would be leaving today, we decided to focus on business talk this morning. She seemed to have a handle on everything and had even done some hiring. After going over last year's figures, I could see we exceeded our forecast. This year was already ahead with the number of bookings than the same period last year.

"Katie, other people in our business are starting to ask questions. They think your absence isn't temporary. Are you coming back soon?"

"In fairness to you, I'm going to say I am. But I'll add the caveat that I'm not sure if I'll stay when I do return to LA."

Kristen didn't look very surprised. "You really like it here, don't you? I sensed it in our video chats, but I had to come out and see for myself. You always seemed the quintessential LA woman to me. You're sure of yourself, comfortable in your own skin. You're smart and creative, building a lucrative and successful business in a very competitive market."

"Keep it coming!" I laughed. "But seriously, you are right. It's such a different pace of life and quality of life here. I'm so torn because I have exerted all my efforts into building KM Party Planners. And I have the most amazing staff, like you, Kristen."

"You need to do what's best for you," Kristen said.

"That sounds simple enough, but what is best? Which place is best? Which situation is best?"

"I've never lived in a small town. It wouldn't be a lifestyle choice for me, but I can see the attraction to it."

Something caught Kristen's eye because she looked

over my shoulder and stopped mid-sentence. "This little town has the added benefit of very friendly and totally hot men."

"Oh, you mean Tyler? He is definitely one of those," I said.

"Well, yes, he is, but here comes another. Hello… cuteness." With a tongue flick to moisten her lips, Kristen smiled at someone standing behind me.

"Good morning," Kristen said.

"And good morning to you. A friend from LA?" Jesse asked.

"Jesse! How nice to see you again. Yes, this is Kristen. Not only a friend, but she's been running my business there while I'm here enjoying your part of the world."

"I'm sorry I couldn't make it yesterday, but I brought some friends over for brunch." Following in the direction he pointed, I saw a couple holding hands and a very attractive blonde. A tiny twinge of disappointment hit me, but I quickly recovered and said, "That's great. I hope you all have a nice time."

"How long will you be in town, Kristen?"

"Leaving today," she said, giving me a kick under the table. "I'm trying to find out when Katie is returning. So many have been asking after her."

"Well, I hope we don't lose her too soon," Jesse said with a wink. "Enjoy the rest of your day."

"Now with men like that around, I know you're not lonely."

"Stop, I'm not ready to date anyone. And what was that kick for?" I asked.

"Oh, nothing," Kristen teased. "I just wanted to make sure you were paying attention. Is that the guy you told me had a fishing lodge up the river? The one with the outdoorsy vibe. And Tyler is definitely the suntanned beach hunk you mentioned. Any more cuties I should know about?"

"Not that I've noticed. After the infamous text breakup, the last thing I need is to start a long-distance romance."

"So that means you're returning to LA. Hooray! We will welcome you with open arms."

"Hold on!" I held my palm up. "Remember, it's the staying there part that I'm still thinking about."

CHAPTER TWENTY

Monday morning, Paddy decided it might be best if he didn't attend the mayor's wake. Word had gotten back to him that Vivian Trimble believed it was Paddy who'd caused her husband's fatal fall. But Maeve knew it wasn't Paddy, and she insisted that she was going to pay her respects. I told her I'd go with her for moral support. She welcomed that but also reached out to her sewing circle friends and timed her arrival at the funeral home to coincide with theirs.

Green Funeral Home was a one-story building set on a modest lot with an ample paved parking line adjacent to it. The red brick facade with white columns exuded the expected solemnity and formality of a funeral home.

As we entered the visitation room for Mayor Trimble, curious gazes followed us. A hush fell over those gathered. Soft classical music played in the background and heavy floral scents from the bouquets and sprays around the casket filled the air. It was strange and unsettling to know we were temporarily the center of attention as we made our way through the room, but soon enough, attention shifted from us and hushed conversations, sniffles, and occasional bursts of laughter as memories of the deceased were shared resumed.

Vivian, her brother, and several others stood near the open casket at the front of the room. Maeve and I joined the slow-moving line of friends and family waiting to share our condolences. When we reached Vivian, she graciously accepted our sympathies and thanked us for coming, before reaching her arms toward the next in line to accept their warm embrace. Her brother simply shook our hands. Then, just like that, we were spit out like widgets from a production line, free to visit with those gathered here.

Maeve headed to join her group of friends seated at chairs at the rear of the room while I walked over to introduce myself to Chief Darnell Jensen. I supposed he was here to both extend his sympathies and to watch the crowd. He leaned casually against the wall in a tucked-away corner. He saw me coming and smiled a greeting.

"Katie Murphy?" he said, extending his hand.

"Yes, but how…?"

"I noticed you Monday morning at the pub and asked Paddy who you were. He is a very proud uncle."

"That's kind of him. We Irish are a tight-knit group."

"Big turnout for Mayor Trimble. Small towns are nice that way. Is there something specific you'd like to talk to me about, Katie?" he asked.

"It's my understanding that my uncle is one of your suspects. If you have any questions for me, I'll be in town for a few more days."

"Thank you for that offer. And I'd like you to know that I have an open-door policy if there's something you'd like to share with me. It's often the random things from unexpected sources that can help solve a crime. I'm a big proponent of the community coming forth with information."

That was a refreshing take on police work, but it caught me off guard. Here I was, thinking I'd offer myself as a character witness, but Darnell's words stopped me. He knew Paddy wasn't guilty, just like I did. But then, who did do it? "Not right here and now, but I appreciate your attitude, and I may show up in your doorway one of these days," I replied.

He let out a low chuckle. "A heads up would assure I'm in. We don't have a big force like LA, so I'm pulled in a lot of directions. But I'd welcome your input just as I have welcomed Paddy's. His experience is invaluable to me. This is difficult not having him to talk things over with." He tipped his hat. "Now ma'am, if you'll excuse me, I'll keep up my…ahem…surveillance."

As I made my way to Aunt Maeve, a short, brisk-moving man approached me. The crisp black suit gave him away as the funeral director. I guessed the bright green tie was a subtle nod to his last name. Despite his serious job, he has a mischievous twinkle in his eye and an infectious grin on his lips. His thinning hair was neatly combed over and showed streaks of silver among the dark strands.

"I just had to introduce myself," he said. "Frederick Green at your service. But you can call me Fred."

"Nice to meet you," I said, finding myself grinning back at him. What a delightful little character.

"I recognize you from your Facebook posts. Your aunt and uncle are such a wonderful addition to our town. We look forward to spending time at our own Seaside Cove public house," he said with emphasis on the last words. "My family has traveled to Ireland several times. We just love it there. Have you ever been to an Irish wake before? I drove right through the middle of one once! It was in a little crossroads village. The pub must have been on one side of the road and the house of the deceased on the other. They might have even had the casket viewing right in their home. I couldn't tell, but the whole thing spilled out into the street. What a sight to behold!"

"I grew up there but don't remember ever seeing a funeral quite like that. Did you get to look around your old building and see what Paddy has done with the place?"

"Oh, my goodness, yes, I did! Quite astounding. If the original plaque with the built date wasn't still among the bricks on the outside wall, I wouldn't have known where I was. And that entire second floor was just amazing to see. Did you know my family lived up there? Who does that to their children?" His belly jiggled as he sought to control his laugh.

"Say you might be able to answer a question I had. Did you ever see a ghost there?"

"Oh yes we did! Yes indeedy. Mrs. McCracken. Molly McCracken. Her husband was the original bank president. My children used her as an excuse for their mischievous actions."

"Like eating all the cookies?" I asked. What a jolly little man for someone in his position.

"Oh yes, and even broken toys. Mr. McCracken's office was up in front, but we usually sensed her more toward the back of the second floor."

His fingers fiddled with the gold chain that held his pocket watch, pulling it out and glancing at it. "Best be off," he said, tucking the watch back into his vest pocket. "There's still much to attend to in the family waiting area. It was a true pleasure to make your acquaintance, Miss Katie Murphy."

The pleasure was all mine, I thought, as he scurried away.

CHAPTER TWENTY-ONE

My last-minute decision to attend the emergency council meeting Monday evening was why I found myself peering at an informational signboard and map. The municipal center was the hub of the town's activities and much larger than I'd imagined a town this size would have. There was a public pool and gymnasium toward the rear of the campus. I picked out the library, police station, and the park department offices on the map.

Still not sure where the meeting would be held, I stopped a woman just leaving the area. She kindly pointed me to the correct building. "There are half a dozen meeting rooms, but you should be able to hear the voices and find the council room. Too bad about the mayor. I heard whispers that he was pushed down the stairs by the man who owns the pub. I'm not sure who can take his place, but I'm glad to hear they are getting right on that important matter."

Alrighty then. It's true. My uncle has a target on his back. The hall smelled of new paint and waxed floors. My footsteps created a high-pitched squeak that echoed down the empty corridor. Since I was late, I hoped to slide into the back and listen. And lucky me, the door was propped open, and only a few in the audience noticed me take a chair close to the back of the room.

The council members were lined up behind a long table at the front of the room and were already far along in their heated discussion about how the mayoral position should be filled. It was easily apparent that they'd never handled anything like this before. Some seemed intent on holding a special election, though the mayor's term was set to end in a few months. Arguments then went back and forth about the cost of a special election when the official one would be coming up soon.

"Couldn't we just let Tim Douglas, our building inspector, manage things until then? He's very knowledgeable and is willing to take on the extra duties," said a member, his knuckles pressed to his cheeks as his elbows leaned on the table. He was the picture of exasperation.

"If you're putting someone in there, it should be our

town clerk. She knows the ins and outs of all the duties." This argument came from a straight-backed woman well into her seventies.

The squabbling continued, but I didn't understand what they finally decided on because my attention was drawn to a hushed conversation happening behind me.

I strained to hear. With the bits and pieces I picked up, the speakers behind me weren't impressed with the tedious and messy way the mayor's position was being filled. A remark implying the next one wouldn't be as crooked as Vinnie's came just as a gavel pounded at the council members' table.

Vinnie? Crooked as Vinnie? Where had I heard that name before? Ah, right, the brief snippet of conversation I heard by the Salty Dawg. Get your gears engaged, Katie Murphy! It had to be Marvin. Mar-vin. Vinnie. So, the happy go-lucky deceased Mayor of Seaside Cove was considered by some as having a questionable character. Definitely mixed opinions about the man.

Paddy stood at a podium facing the council. He thanked the members for agreeing to add his point of business to the evening's agenda. "I've emailed all of you my paperwork. If you'll allow me, I'd like to put an overhead map up on the screen. It might help you understand how I've addressed the objections that were previously brought up."

Several members shuffled in their seats before one spoke.

"Mr. Murphy, I believe we are all in agreement that the parking accommodations you presented to us are adequate to allow you to use the additional banquet space you have on the second floor. Mr. Nicolas Drake submitted a letter earlier saying he had no more issues with your parking plans. I see Mr. Kane in the audience. Are you here to protest Mr. Murphy's parking plans again?"

One of the men I'd overheard talking behind me stood. A five-o-clock scruffy shadow covered his chin hair, giving him a rugged appearance. He wasn't tall, but his muscular frame and the look in his eyes held a hint of danger, giving him a don't challenge me appearance.

"Nah. I think it's fine." And that was it. Mr. Kane sat down.

"Looks like you can go ahead, Paddy. And may we congratulate you on a successful opening day. Meeting adjourned."

I thought Paddy had noticed me because he was making a beeline in my direction, but instead, he passed my row of chairs to reach out and shake Mr. Kane's hand.

"Thank you, Butch. I really appreciate you coming here tonight. If you'd not been here in person, they probably would have had to write you a registered letter and all that malarky."

"Happy to do it, man. Nic and I both apologize for giving you grief about it, to begin with." He cleared his throat before leaning closer to Paddy. "I hate to admit this, but we were being pressured. We owe you an apology. Had you pegged all wrong, buddy. Best of luck to you."

"Please stop in and let me buy you one," Paddy said.

"I might just take you up on that someday."

Tonight went better than planned for Paddy. With the parking issue settled, all the problems with the pub were finally cleared up.

Or so I thought.

CHAPTER TWENTY-TWO

It was noon when I drove downtown to the pub. My plans were to try their salmon fish cakes for lunch, then maybe head out to the beach to finish up my E.L. Brooks book. But my mind was torn. There had to be something I could do about the investigation. Especially after what I heard last night. If Butch Kane felt pressured by someone to make trouble for Paddy, it had to have been a pretty serious thing. He didn't look like the kind of man to let just anything or anyone force him to do something. Putting that together with the conversation I'd overheard outside the Salty Dawg, the mayor, AKA Vinnie, owed him something. Who was putting the pressure on Butch?

Soon as I'd settled into a small booth, Liam approached me with a concerned look on his face.

"What's up with Paddy today? He was excited to get on last night's agenda for his parking permit. Do you know if it went through?"

"It sailed through without an issue. I haven't seen him yet today, so I'm not sure. Maeve didn't mention anything this morning. Is he here now?"

"He's up in his office, I think," Liam answered. "Are you heading back to LA soon?"

"Probably by the weekend. I'll see. I hate to leave with this unsolved murder investigation hanging over us all," I said.

"So, it is a murder then?" Liam shook his head slowly. "Unbelievable. Here in this little town and in Paddy's Pub. Do you know if they have any suspects?"

"I don't know. The Chief of Police here is a pretty cool guy. He said he wanted to hear of anything someone saw or heard," I said. "You know, I'm thinking I might talk to Slim after lunch and ask him a couple of questions about that night."

"Slim told me he had a long interview with the chief. Even thought he might be a suspect himself in the chief's eyes, he said his alibi of going to the Salty Dawg that night was verified by a couple of people." Liam noticed some new customers had entered the pub. "Look, I have to get back to work. Catch you later."

With a nervous stomach, I finished my lunch and

took the back stairway up to Paddy's office. As I passed the kitchen, I poked my head in to ask Slim if I could talk to him later. He gave me a quick nod.

Paddy sat slumped behind his desk, staring out the window. His view was absolutely amazing. The river emptying into the cove. Seagulls and pelicans sailing overhead. Sailboats in the marina, their masts gently swaying and clanging. But by his posture, I bet Paddy wasn't even seeing the beauty there.

He startled when I spoke his name, spinning in his chair and sitting upright. "Well, hello. There you are. Sorry I didn't stay for morning coffee. I had it here earlier with my friends. What are you up to today?"

Trying to read through his demeanor of all is normal, I felt the undercurrent Liam had brought up.

"Lazy day for me," I said. "Mind if I take a seat and enjoy your view for a second?" I grabbed a chair, not giving him a chance to answer. "All your opening problems are over. The parking issue was the last one, right?"

"You were there and heard them clear that up."

"I was. Then why so glum?"

He dropped his eyes, nervously rubbing his fingers. "It's not the last issue."

"Care to explain why it isn't?" I leaned in hoping he'd share his concerns with me. It hurt me to see him so dejected. Maybe I could help somehow.

"Sure you want to listen to this old man's troubles? I would think you've had your fill of it by now," he said.

"Paddy, tell me. Maybe I can help."

"I really doubt it, but I'll let you know because soon I'll have to tell everyone."

He paused.

I waited.

The phone rang and he grabbed for it. From my end of the conversation, it seemed it was his insurance agent. He handled the call and hung up. He busied himself, reaching for paper to make a note but not getting back to our conversation.

"Paddy, what is wrong?"

Without looking up, he kept writing. "The bank is calling my construction loan." He stood and put the paper in a filing cabinet folder, keeping his back to me.

"And isn't that the normal thing they would do when you're done with construction?"

"Yes, and it was set up to automatically transfer to a normal business loan." Paddy turned to face me and his voice choked. "But that isn't happening, Katie. I'm afraid I'm going to lose this all."

"Now hold on. Why? Give me an explanation," I said, grappling to absorb what he said. Something was off about it. It couldn't be true.

He looked up with tired eyes. "With all the delays I've

had, they kept extending the loan, which is perfectly fine. There were no red flags. No missed payments. The loan committee just couldn't see extending it again. That they have unique pressures. Nor could they see their way to increasing my line of credit to cover it. I've been told it's gone on way too long, and then they mentioned the murder in the building."

"Hold on now, Paddy. What does that have to do with your business finances?"

"That's the very question I asked. But with a pompous attitude he said it was a business decision and didn't directly answer me or give me any further information." Paddy's expression was painful to see. The uncertainty in his voice hard to hear. "I chose the small local bank because of the personal, community touch they promoted. Was that a poor decision?"

Paddy looked so very crushed, his head dropping into his hands. I moved to give him a small, comforting hug.

With a catch in his voice, he said, "I have two days to come up with the money or else…"

CHAPTER TWENTY-THREE

What a kick in the gut!

Even I have to admit that the timing of this seems awfully suspicious. The construction issues were solved. The parking issues were resolved.

But the murder was unsolved.

Could a bank really make a financial decision based on that? Like Paddy, I thought that community banks would be more than willing to work with small businesses and issues that arose.

The opening was a great success…wait…that might be the reason! Was it truly a bank decision, or was someone still pulling strings to sabotage Paddy? Someone who wanted to see Paddy's Pub close? Who would want him to fail? And why would anyone want him to fail? It seemed to circle back to the mayor's murder.

Last night Butch's words might have more to do with this than I thought. Someone doesn't want Paddy to succeed. Someone murdered Marvin, AKA Vinnie. Same person or different person? It would kill two birds with one stone if Paddy was found guilty now. Could I change that? I had to try.

Downstairs, I joined Slim while he took his break. After a few pleasantries, I encouraged him to tell me everything he knew about the mayor's murder. Without going into the new stumbling block with the bank loan, I told Slim that someone was still messing with my uncle and if the murderer could be found, it might take the pressure off of him.

With hesitation, Slim began with a frank admission. "Your uncle isn't alone. I'm a suspect too."

Wait. This was getting so mixed up. "But didn't you have an alibi?"

"Yeah, well, I do, but not a very strong one. And until someone confesses and is charged, I was told not to leave the area. And I get it. I have a key to the pub, and that's one critical, undeniable part of the whole thing. Along with the fact that I was there that night. And I could have a motive."

"What motive would you possibly have?"

"I used to work at Bayview. The staff there called me a disgruntled employee. That I complained about being treated unfairly. Play that ahead, and the scenario comes up that the mayor threatened to disparage me to Paddy or some nonsense like that. None of it's true, but what am I to do? The more I protest against that sort of stuff, the guiltier I look."

"Ah, I get it. It's hard to prove things when other voices are saying the opposite. I heard the Bayview restaurant isn't doing so well."

"You heard right ma'am. But it wasn't my doing. I just didn't want to work there. I don't talk bad about places or people, but I'll do anything to help your uncle. He's one of the good ones."

Now I'm getting really steamed. Slim is right. Paddy is good. I don't know who is behind all this, but if I can clear Paddy's name in forty-eight hours, the bank might consider extending the loan. If they think there is pressure on them now…why I'll show them pressure!

"Slim, do you by any chance know Butch Kane? He owns the Salty Dawg."

"Yes, ma'am, I sure do."

"He was at the council meeting last night and said something that caught my attention. That he'd misjudged Paddy. I'd like to find out more about what he meant."

"He's a unique dude. You'd stick out like a sore thumb if you went to the Salty Dawg yourself. But hey, I'm heading over there after I get off work tonight. You could come with me then," Slim said.

"That's a good thought. Go right to the source," I said. "Is he usually around?"

"It's hit or miss."

"I'll take you up on your offer, but don't go just because of me," I said.

Slim's lips curved into a bashful smile as he glanced downward with a shy expression. "Now don't laugh, but this old guy is kind of sweet on the bartender there."

"Slim, that's so cute. And you aren't old at all."

"Old enough to be your father," he quickly pointed out. "But not too old to enjoy the ladies."

With a chuckle, I said, "What time are you off work here?"

CHAPTER TWENTY-FOUR

It was clear Slim had put on extra cologne for this outing. He'd swapped out his T-shirt for a slightly rumpled plaid shirt. He was upping his game. Slim was in love or at least deeply infatuated.

The Salty Dawg's neon signs could be seen from blocks away. One sign flickered, casting a pulsing light onto the windows of the bar. The letters seemed to dance and blur as they flickered on and off, making it difficult to read the words and giving the place a worn and dingy appearance. A handful of motorcycles and pickup trucks were parked off to the side of the building. Several small fishing craft were tied up on the old dock at the river's edge, ghostly in the dim light of the moon.

A sense of scrutiny descended upon us as soon as

Slim and I stepped through the door. Eyes flicked toward us, and the stillness of their stares unsettled me. But if the bar's patrons were curious about me, it was obvious they were comfortable with Slim as they quietly returned to looking up at the television, shooting another ball on the pool table, or taking a sip of their drink.

Slim found us two stools in the far corner of the bar. Their faux leather seats were veined with thin cracks. The stools wobbled unevenly as I sat down and hooked my heels in the frame. I rolled my shoulders, trying to calm myself and appear casual, at ease.

Looking around the room, I didn't see Butch. But then what would I even have to say to him? Hey big guy, I overheard someone threatening someone else outside in your parking lot a couple weeks ago. Got anything to say about that? From the little I'd seen of Butch, I found it hard to imagine he'd engage in conversation with me over those comments.

The bartender, a woman in her mid-fifties, her once vibrant red hair now faded and pulled back into a messy bun, gave off an air of confidence as she worked with purpose and efficiency. There was also a hint of exhaustion in her gaze as if she'd been dealing with it all for far too long. She wore a Salty Dawg T-shirt and jeans. Her face, weathered by the harsh Florida sun, still showed signs of her former beauty.

At the sight of Slim, a smile lit up her face. However, it quickly faded as she turned her gaze toward me, and a mask of suspicion crossed her face. He was quick to introduce us and make it clear that I was not his date but just the niece of his boss. He told Ruby that I had some questions for Butch.

"He's not here," she said in a voice raspy from years of smoking. "The usual draft for you, Slim?"

When he nodded, she turned to me. "What can I get you?"

To fit in here, I whimsically ordered a shot and the same beer as Slim. I'd seen that done in the movies at places like this. But when she asked me what kind of shot, I wasn't sure. Whiskey was the first liquor that popped into my head. It seemed to be the right answer because she turned away to get our drinks.

While Ruby was gone, I took the chance to ask Slim if he came here often.

"I do because I like to frequent places where you don't have to keep up a pretense. People here don't constantly boast about their perfect lives or pry into yours. And if they do ask, you don't feel obligated to share. Keepin' it simple is best for me."

"Maeve has told me that you are an excellent chef. How'd you learn all that?"

"I was in the Navy and ended up working on a base where I was trained in serving the top brass. Found out I liked it, and it kinda came naturally to me. I stayed in until I aged out. I get a nice pension but work to keep busy. Keep myself occupied so I don't get into trouble," Slim said with a grin.

"So that's where the tattoos come from?" I asked.

"Most of them," he said with a shrug. He rolled his sleeve up and pointed to one that he'd done recently while I took his arm to move it further into the light.

"Very nice. I'm not into tattoos but I'm sure seeing more of them in the past few years. Not just for sailors anymore." I felt Ruby's eyes on me, so I let go of Slim's arm. Better not to get her ire up because I'd decided Ruby could answer a couple of questions for me since Butch wasn't here.

"I'm glad Ruby likes tattoos," Slim said. "She has a couple of them herself. What is it you wanted to talk to Butch about?"

"On the Friday night before the mayor's body was found, I was out for an evening walk. As I passed by the Salty Dawg, I overheard a threatening conversation. There were two men in the shadows of the building, and they didn't see me. This one guy, who might have worked here because he had just carried out a bag of garbage, relayed a message to the other guy who he called Junior, that Butch wanted what Vinnie owed him. Then the guy called Junior, claimed he's not Vinnie's boy anymore. There was some scuffling and shoving. The next words I heard were Junior asking for more time."

"You want Butch to clear this all up for you?" Slim looked slowly around the bar before he leaned in close to me. "You'd better be careful, Katie. Like I said, the people here aren't real forthcoming with information like that. But I can help you with one thing. Marvin Trimble used to go by the nickname of Vinnie. Junior, I don't know. You could ask Ruby."

"You just confirmed my guess as to who Vinnie was, but I think it might be better if you ask Ruby about Junior," I suggested, afraid she might not be receptive to my prying into her customers' business.

Slim got the hint, and when Ruby made it back with our beers, he asked if she knew someone by the nickname of Junior.

"Who wants to know?"

"I do."

"You and who else?" Ruby asked, staring at me with her intense green eyes.

"Katie does. You can trust her."

"Ain't about trust. Folk in here don't like questions being asked about them," Ruby said. "Your friend here is asking for a reason. And unless it's a really good reason, whether I like someone or don't like them, I don't just share information 'bout them."

They both turned to me with questioning looks. Now how do I handle this?

"Ruby, I'm going to be totally upfront with you. You probably know the deceased Mayor Trimble or Vinnie." I felt if I used his nickname, it might soften her up to be more open to my next question.

She said, "Of course I know him. He used to come in here quite a bit, but not as much as before because now he had an image to keep up. Married up to the rich lady and being our mayor and all. Thought we weren't classy enough for the circles he moved in now."

I put myself out on a limb that might be cut off behind me if what I was about to say wasn't true. "Vinnie owed Butch. My uncle is being accused of Vinnie's murder. I thought maybe Butch or this Junior guy would know something that might help us."

"Us?"

I looked toward Slim, not wanting to put him in a tough spot.

"Ruby, remember how I was telling you I found the body and had a key and all that stuff?" Slim said.

Ruby nodded and cocked her head. "Sure, but what's that have to do with her?"

"She's trying to find out anything that would help show who murdered the mayor. It would take the heat off me too," Slim said.

"So now you're telling me you're part of some investigating team? Yeah right."

This wasn't going well. "It's okay, Slim. Thanks for trying."

Surprisedly Ruby's defensive edge dropped away as fast as it had appeared. "You two might be on to something."

While using a towel to wipe the bar surface between us, she slowly looked around, before propping her forearms on the bar and leaning in. Her voice was low and steady. "I know exactly who Junior is."

CHAPTER TWENTY-FIVE

Wednesday morning, Winnie, Maeve, and I were enjoying a peaceful conversation on the front porch when we suddenly heard Paddy's heavy footsteps approaching. He came barreling through the screen door, his phone already in hand as he thrust it toward me.

An anonymous text on his cell phone screen read *hope she enjoyed her shot and beer but warn that nosy redhead that she's making more trouble for you.* Yikes…my mind raced. Who knew I'd been at the Salty Dawg last night, and better yet, who cared enough to send this threat to him?

"A shot and a beer?" The question spat out of Paddy's mouth. "What on earth are you up to?"

Trying to keep him calm, I handed his phone back

and said, "I didn't even realize you could send texts anonymously."

"Don't try to get around giving me an answer, missy."

"No biggie. Slim and I were just talking yesterday. He was going to see his girlfriend, who works at the Salty Dawg, and he invited me along. I just thought it would be a small-town adventure for a big-city girl."

"Big-city girl, hah? Well, someone obviously thought it was not as innocent as you make it sound. What happened at that bar? I'm going to give Slim a piece of my mind for putting you in danger."

"C'mon, Paddy," Maeve said. "She's a good lass, and Slim is a grand fella. Sure, he might be a bit rough around the edges, but he'd never take her to a place where she wasn't safe."

"Salty Dawg after dark is no playground," Paddy snapped. "What happened there, Katie?"

"Salty Dawg?" Winnie drawled. "Their motorcycle club raised the most for our Toys for Tots last Christmas. Say, are y'all going to put out a box at the pub for next year? Your location would be excellent for fundraising stuff. I'll be hitting you up for a few things like that. But sweetie, your uncle is right. You best be careful. There is a certain edge at that place, and they don't take kindly to strangers."

"Okay everyone. I get it. But remember I'm not a

child and I've lived in a big city. I think I have enough common sense and street smarts by now. The place is not in some crime-ridden neighborhood. But I will admit I must have stirred something up for you to receive that threatening text. For that I am sorry, Uncle Paddy. You don't need any more troubles."

"No kidding. Just leave it to the law. Or are you thinkin' Darnell is not doing a proper job?" Paddy glared at me. "He will get it right. Don't be puttin' yourself in danger. If something happened to you while you're staying here with us, I could never look my family in the eye again."

"Of course, I don't think that about Darnell. I know he wants this solved, but it's not the only thing on his plate, Paddy. If you'll hear me out, it might help your case," I said.

Winnie added, "You know how the authorities always ask for the public's help. She's the public. Let her help."

Maeve nudged him to answer me too. "She's right. Darnell will take any help he can. He doesn't know what he doesn't know."

"There's something I can't seem to keep straight," I said. "You went out again late on Sunday night. But what time did you get home?"

"I'm not sure. What does it matter?" Paddy said.

"Because you were probably there at the time of death. Surely Darnell asked you these questions. I'm putting together clues and trying to make connections. What you know might help fill in some gaps for me. In fact it might help me to figure out who sent that text to you about me being at the bar. I think I have the right to know that don't you?"

Winnie stomped her foot down on the porch floor. "I think you need to know. It's your honor at stake."

I had to laugh at her drama. My honor? "Well not quite that far, Winnie. But if there's someone stalking me…"

"You stuck out like a sore thumb," Paddy interrupted. "Anyone would have noticed you."

"And about that time?" I asked again, not appreciating him deviating back to my being at the Dawg.

"Fine. It was after midnight, around twelve-thirty, when I locked up and left," Paddy said, stuffing his phone back in his pocket. "And Maeve, I'm sorry you've been dragged into this. I finally confessed to Darnell about being there late into the night."

"And you turned on the new alarm?"

"Yes, I did. I remember that clearly because Sammy had just showed it to me."

"Sammy was there with you until twelve-thirty?"

"No." Paddy rubbed his forehead and walked over to

lean on the porch railing and look toward the street. "When I went in earlier in the day after we got back from the beach, Sammy wasn't done and told me he was going to have to get something to eat and would finish up later no matter how long it took. I asked him to text me when he was done with the alarm he was installing because I wanted to see it and make sure he gave me directions on how to set it, the code and all that."

"Look at me Paddy," Maeve said. "No more fudging or not giving me the complete story. So that was why you left again later on Sunday night, because he texted you that he was done?"

"Right. He showed me how to change the code and work the system on my computer and phone. All that stuff."

"Paddy, think now. What would set off the alarm?" I asked.

"Opening the two doors and a few ground-floor windows that are operational."

"How long was Sammy there after you went through the alarm instructions?" The timing here was critical. Even though Paddy was explaining things the best he could, I needed to clarify the exact order of things as they happened on that awful night.

"He left right after he was done talking to me. He was very tired, but he confided in me that he owed me for all the delays his work and his employees had caused, and he was glad the work was done now."

"Why didn't you just come home then?" Maeve interrupted. "Why did you stay?"

"We both noticed lights left on upstairs, so I told Sammy I'd go up to shut them off and then ended up staying to do some work in the office." Paddy nervously rubbed his hands. "I was still wound up and needed to catch up on some paperwork, so I decided I'd get it out of the way."

"And you never heard anything strange?" I asked. "Or sensed anyone prowling around?"

"I didn't. Believe me, I would have remembered that."

I tried to get him to focus by walking to him where he stood and holding his eyes. "Paddy, during all this time, has anything come to mind that would have put the mayor in your building after twelve-thirty that night? The window of time means it could have happened while you were there or after you left. You must know how important this is. Try. Try to remember."

In a confused, puzzled, and exasperated voice, Paddy said, "I cannot. That's what is keeping me up at night. Why was the mayor in the pub, and who was there with him? If it had just been him, the fall could have been an accident. But with the blow to the head like the medical examiner found, it meant he wasn't there alone." And with that he stepped back away from me. "If you're done with the questions, I need to get to work."

As Paddy climbed into his golf cart, I called out, "And I'll have you know I've done shots before."

Paddy took off without replying.

"Girl, don't know what you were doing at that bar, but I suspect it has something to do with helping your uncle," Winnie said. "You got some guts. If I was in his shoes, I'd be mighty grateful for any help I could get. He don't show it, but I bet he is too. Now, I gotta skedaddle on outta here myself."

"More volunteering?" Maeve asked as she moved to pick up our glasses.

"Yep. Today it's the hospital."

"I didn't know you were volunteering there. Good for you. Are you a Candy Striper?" Maeve asked.

"Oh lordy! No!" Winnie snorted, almost choking on her words. "This old broad in a cute little pink and white striped apron. I think not! I volunteer on the coffee cart."

"What are Candy Stripers?" I asked.

Both Maeve and Winnie spun to look at me. "See there, Maeve, the young ones don't even know what that is nowadays. It's a word for hospital volunteers, usually like forty or fifty years younger than me and that many years ago." Winnie chuckled.

"And they wore cute little dresses or, like Winnie said, aprons. With pink and white stripes," Maeve answered. "So sweet. But I'm taking off too. You coming down to the pub today, Katie? I'm trying out a new dessert. Irish Cream Cheesecake."

"That's awfully tempting, but I first wanted to take a walk and clear my head."

"See you later," Maeve said. "And Katie, please watch your back. It's daylight in Seaside Cove, but evil doesn't need darkness."

CHAPTER TWENTY-SIX

My mind raced as I set off. I didn't have time for a leisurely stroll. My feet moved with purpose and determination as I made my way toward the police station. Paddy's text message had been serious. It had to be connected to what Ruby had revealed to me last night. I needed more information. As I pushed through the doors of the lobby, my eyes immediately fell upon Hannah, talking and laughing with a young female officer behind the front desk. She must be one of her contacts here. Maybe she's the Blaire mentioned by the chief at the murder scene.

As soon as Hannah saw her smile dropped. "Katie, are you okay? You look flustered."

I didn't want to start spilling my questions here in the lobby, so I blamed it on my fast-paced walk here.

"I just dropped off a few newspapers for the staff. Blaire, this is Katie Murphy. Her aunt and uncle just opened the new Irish pub."

"Nice to meet you. Do you live here in town now?" Blaire asked.

"No. I live out on the West Coast." I didn't like being abrupt, but I wasn't up for chit-chat either.

"Hope you're enjoying your visit. Is there something we can help you with?" Blaire asked.

"Yes, I have to talk to Chief Darnell." There were so many pieces to the situation surrounding the mayor's murder and the urgency was building especially after the text Paddy had gotten. Did someone at the Dawg find out I'd overheard that earlier conversation?

"Certainly. He's with someone in his office right now, but if you'd like to take a seat, I don't expect him to be long."

"Sure thanks. Hannah, could you join me for a sec?"

We found a quiet spot on a bench near the windows. I spoke in a low voice. "Is Blaire your contact here?"

"You figured it out, Katie. She's my younger cousin. I try not to bother her or get her in trouble by asking all sorts of questions, but she's good at shutting me down if I get too pushy."

"So has your cousin mentioned any more news on the investigation?" I asked.

"Nothing new really. But she said the chief is not ready to charge anyone, and it's been over a week."

"Do you know if he has other suspects?" I asked.

"Chief's been pretty closed mouth whenever I've asked him to give some progress on his investigation to put in the paper. But I've thought about it and have done a bit of investigating myself. After all, I'm pretty much the only hard-hitting journalist in the county." She blew on her knuckle and burnished her chest. "Want to hear who I think the two suspects might be?"

"Sure. I'm all ears."

"I believe that both Sammy Baker, the electrical contractor, and Tim Douglas, the building inspector, are because they've butted heads with the mayor repeatedly and would have had access to the pub."

"Interesting. Have you told Chief Darnell about your idea?" I asked.

"Yep, and he took down the information I gave him. Do you want to hear about my reasoning?"

"I do, but first, can I ask you a question, Hannah? Last night I heard that the mayor married up. What did that mean? Was Vivian's family wealthy?"

"I don't know much about the Fagan family history, but my mother-in-law would. She's old stock here. Are you thinking trouble in the marriage? They always say look at the spouse first."

CHAPTER TWENTY-SEVEN

After being told by Blaire that the chief was ready to meet with me, I didn't have time to discuss Hannah's theories on the murderer's identity.

"Welcome to my office, Ms. Murphy. Please take a seat."

"Thank you, Chief."

"What can I do for you?"

"I wanted to take you up on your offer to speak with you. Can I run a few things by you?"

"I am always open to input," the chief said. "I don't claim to know everything."

"Then I'll jump right in. You got the call about a body at Paddy's Pub at four forty-five AM from Slim who'd opened the kitchen for a delivery."

"That's right."

"And then this little dog comes walking up to him. Slim figured the dog had gotten in somehow and made himself at home for the night. He checked the dog's tag and called the phone number on it, and lo-and-behold, he hears a phone ringing somewhere in the pub. That's when he found the body and called the police."

"Correct."

I pushed on. "My uncle told me that three people had keys. That's important."

"But certainly not limiting. Construction sites are vulnerable because they are often unsecured with workers going in and out. Did you know that one of the contractors reported thefts of his tools a couple months ago? And then there are just the nosy folk who poke around construction sites. Which I've considered the reason the mayor was even there. He likes to be out and about town, walking his dog at all hours of the night. Restless sort of soul he was."

"I heard there may have been a drinking problem with him in the past. Did Vivian report him missing that night?"

"No, she doesn't do that anymore. She used to, and we'd often find him at one of the bars. It seems he has gotten his drinking under control now."

"But why didn't she call in if her husband wasn't home at four in the morning? It seems odd, doesn't it?"

"I asked her about it and she claimed she had fallen asleep."

"And you believed her?"

The chief gave me a stern look, suggesting I was crossing a line. He seemed receptive to my questions so far and I didn't want to lose that. At this point did it matter if Vivian was sleeping or just not calling around looking for her husband. "I'm sorry if I'm being too pushy here, but I know my uncle is still a suspect and well...he's very important to me. Do you think the mayor had fallen off the wagon?"

"It crossed my mind finding him like that in a pub. It would have been a shame. But when the coroner found the contusion on the back of his head and determined it was highly unlikely to have occurred during the fall, well, it didn't matter if he was drunk because most likely the blow to the head killed him."

"Did he also gamble when he was drinking?"

"I'm sure he did. He has a bit of a sketchy past, but like I said, he seemed to have gotten past all of that with his marriage and then winning the mayoral election."

"And Mrs. Trimble's response at the scene was appropriate?"

"Vivian can be a judgmental person, but she has a soft spot for her husband. She certainly seemed broken up. Why do you ask that?"

"The old suspect the spouse thing, I guess."

"I've wanted to respect her period of mourning and all, but I really need to have a longer interview with her as well. She seems to be resistant to it. But now that you're here, can I ask you a question?"

"I'll answer anything I can to help clear Paddy's name. Oh, and now to find the murderer. Let me share one more thing, please. This is my uncle's personal business, and I'm asking you to keep it to yourself, but I think it may have something to do with this case. I think you should know about it." I explained the situation with the construction loan being called by the bank and that Paddy was given forty-eight hours to clear his name or repay the loan. "So, to clear his name, the murderer has to be found."

Even as I said the words it felt like I'd been punched in the gut. Who was causing all the troubles for Uncle Paddy. He'd looked so depressed and defeated when he told me about the bank. The feeling that I was getting closer to the truth might also mean there was someone out there who knew it and would do anything to stop me. But now I had to convince Darnell to work together with me.

"Very interesting, Katie. I appreciate you bringing that to me. But back to my question for you. I'd like to hear about what you were doing at the Salty Dawg last night and what it has to do with the threatening text your uncle received this morning."

Paddy must have told him about the threatening text. Choosing my words carefully so as not to make myself appear as a renegade wanna-be detective, I told him about the overheard conversation outside the Salty Dawg and then what I picked up from my visit there last night.

"You could be on to something," Darnell said. "You need to be careful, Katie."

CHAPTER TWENTY-EIGHT

On the way back to the pub, I was actually relieved that Paddy had taken that text to Darnell. The police should know about it. I was glad I'd been pressured to get my sleuthing out in the open. But had I done more to hurt Paddy than help him?

My next destination was the First National Bank of Seaside Cove. I knew Paddy would refuse my offer to help him, so I wasn't going to ask. Sometimes it's better to ask forgiveness than permission, especially to do what I felt had to be done. In talking with Paddy, he let slip approximately how much he owes on the construction loan. It seemed manageable.

Since there is a risk that the crime won't be solved by tomorrow, I've decided I will pay it off and surprise Paddy and Maeve. The large glass doors of the First

National Bank of Seaside Cove opened silently as I walked up.

The greeter escorted me to a Ms. Haberkorn, who might be able to help me with a loan payoff. After I explained who I was and what I hoped to be able to do, she spent a couple of minutes telling me in her sweet Southern drawl that she had attended the opening and how much she loved Paddy's Pub. Then she took a few moments looking at her computer screen and clicking the keyboard.

A puzzled expression appeared on her face before she said, "There's a flag on this. Could you excuse me for a moment while I take this to my superior to make certain that there isn't a problem with closing out the loan?"

Gosh, I'd hoped I could keep this simple and surprise Paddy. He could use some good news. Then I could get back to figuring out who might have wanted to put this added pressure on him and how it figured in with what I'd learned.

She seemed to be gone a long time. It was rather sloppy and quite unprofessional of her to leave her computer open. I turned and looked through the interior window to the lobby. I couldn't see where she'd gone. Dare I?

Oh look! Isn't that a lovely African violet on the

credenza behind her desk? And her winter cactus is in full bloom. I must step over there, behind her desk, and take a closer look at them.

It only took a matter of seconds to scan the computer screen and see the details of the flag on the loan. Luckily, I caught sight of Ms. Haberkorn approaching just in time to smile and compliment her on her green thumb and ask a few questions about how she did it before I returned to my seat.

"I think you'll be pleased to learn that my supervisor cleared the way for you to pay off the loan. Isn't that great? And aren't you just the sweetest to do this for your aunt and uncle? You must be quite the business-woman yourself to just have these funds transferred over here and be able to save the day for Paddy's Pub!"

I watched as she took the information I'd given her to accept the wire transfer from my Los Angeles bank and within a short period of time, we were done.

"Thank you so much Ms. Haberkorn. I'll be sure to let my uncle know how helpful you've been."

"You're welcome, Katie. It was nice to meet you," she said. 'Would you like a clipping from my African violet?"

It took me just a heartbeat to realize what she meant. "Ah no, but thank you very much. I'm afraid I'd kill it."

CHAPTER TWENTY-NINE

As I walked back to the pub, a stroke of luck came my way. Eve Brooks was browsing through books at the Main Street bookstore. It was the perfect opportunity to ask her about the Fagan family and gather more information, just as Hannah had suggested. I knew she would be willing to help, given the interest she showed when I gave her a tour of the pub last Friday. After she finished her purchases, I caught her at the door and invited her to join me on a nearby bench. I shared all that I knew about the situation with Mayor Trimble's murder, trying to piece together a cohesive storyline that made sense. I concluded by explaining what I saw at the bank earlier that day.

"Katie, you've presented a very compelling explanation for the night of the murder, including motive and means. But if what you say is true, it may be difficult to prove," Eve said.

I nodded in agreement. She had me there. "I know. And there are still issues with the timing. There's got to be a way to figure that out. The window of time given for the time of death conflicts with the time the alarm was reset. How to explain someone getting out of the building without triggering the alarm. All of it feels like it should fit. It should work out."

Eve placed a comforting hand on my arm. "Don't worry, I think I can help with that. I have to head home now to finish some work and get ready for dinner with Vivian tonight. But I'll speak with Chief Darnell and hopefully tie up these loose ends."

"Really? So, you think I might be right?"

"I do, Katie. You've done an impressive job connecting the pieces so far. Let me take it from here."

"Should I tell Paddy and Maeve everything?" I asked.

"It would be best to wait," Eve advised.

Later that evening, Eve called me to give me an update. It was still a sleepless night for me, but her words confirmed that she had definitely advanced the ball.

Now to get the final pieces to fall into place.

CHAPTER THIRTY

This morning was the forty-eight-hour break point for the loan issue. Did the paperwork on the payoff come together at the bank yesterday? If it did, at least that worry would be lifted off Paddy and Maeve's shoulders, and they could move forward knowing the pub was not at risk of foreclosure.

Busying myself with wiping down the Coffee Corner tables for the third time, I tried to put the loan off my mind, but then that brain space was filled with thoughts about what Darnell and Eve had accomplished last night. The chief had texted me earlier with the wonderful news that he wanted to deliver to Paddy and Maeve personally.

"You look as nervous as a long-tailed cat in a room

full of rocking chairs," Winnie said as she bit into her warm caramel roll.

"She's right," Maeve said. "Shouldn't you go get that oil change on your car taken care of? Don't wait until the last minute. You don't want any car trouble on your drive back to Los Angeles tomorrow."

"I'm not leaving town until Saturday now. It'll be fine." My sideways glances out the window didn't help calm me at all.

Paddy was going over food and drink orders with Slim and Liam at one of the tables. A small group of local school bus drivers sat by the front window, enjoying the angle of the morning sun coming through. Already Paddy's Pub was enjoying regular customers.

When the bus drivers called out greetings, all our eyes turned toward the entry where Chief Darnell stood with a man in a black suit.

Breathe, Katie.

It's finally going to happen. I thought I was safe in assuming the suit guy was with the bank. Fingers crossed that he brought good news, too.

"Morning Paddy. Maeve," Darnell said. "I think you know Mr. Lawrence Harvey from our fine local bank."

Paddy stood to shake hands with Lawrence, a look of resignation on his face. I had a moment of regret that I hadn't let him know this was happening, but until the wire transfer was completed and the paperwork was finalized, I didn't want to get his hopes up.

"Paddy, my friend, I think you should take a seat. Mr. Harvey has some news for you," Darnell said.

Paddy gathered himself, saying he'd rather stand as he was expecting the worst, but quickly collapsed back into his seat when he heard the news.

"Mr. And Mrs. Murphy, I'd like to present the paperwork showing that your construction loan with the First National Bank of Seaside Cove has been paid in full. Congratulations and my sincere apology for what has transpired at the bank."

Mr. Harvey handed Paddy a folder, which he pulled to his lips before holding it tight against his chest while Maeve screamed, wildly clapping her hands.

"How can this be?" Paddy exclaimed, looking around at everyone with glistening eyes.

What overwhelming feelings of relief he must be having. My heart was full of love for both of them and gratitude that I was able to provide this help.

Darnell looked to me. "I believe your niece Katie can explain that in greater detail, Paddy. But why I'm here is because I wanted to personally deliver some good news to you. With help from your family and friends, the murderer of Mayor Trimble has confessed and is, as we speak, sitting in our jail awaiting arraignment on charges of first-degree murder."

Maeve broke out with a sob and Winnie shouted, "Lord have mercy," before raising her hands to the sky.

No one but me seemed to notice that we'd been joined by Vivian and Eve, who'd quietly slipped in and heard the two announcements. Eve smiled and nodded before turning toward Vivian and squeezing her shoulder. It appeared she was giving her a nudge to speak.

"And I am eternally grateful that justice will be served, even though…" Vivian paused to gather herself as her dear friend Eve reached out a hand to support her. "Even though the man charged with murder is my own brother, Brian Fagan."

The room was filled with gasps, even from the bus drivers. Maeve quickly ran to hug both Vivian and Eve tightly before running to Mr. Harvey for an awkward embrace. Meanwhile, Darnell welcomed her with outstretched arms.

Maeve's next stop was me. She reached up to embrace me. "Ah, my Katie girl. What have you done?"

"I'll tell you later, Aunt Maeve," I whispered to her, then turned to the banker. "Thank you, Mr. Lawrence, for personally delivering this news to my aunt and uncle. How about we all sit down with a cup of coffee, or tea, if you prefer? Between us all gathered here, I'm sure we can explain everything to Paddy and Maeve."

As I set up pastry plates, I noticed the bus drivers had to depart for their kindergarten routes, but they paused to shake Darnell's hand and offer their congratulations on the exciting news. It was only a matter of time before word spread throughout Seaside Cove.

CHAPTER THIRTY-ONE

Everyone else accepted my invitation to listen to more of the story. Winnie hustled around taking orders, and Maeve manned the coffee maker while I got out napkins and dessert plates. When we all were settled, Darnell suggested I begin the story of how this all came together.

"My first thought when my Uncle Paddy got the news on Tuesday that his construction loan was going to be called was that there could be someone else who wanted to see Paddy's Pub fail. First, the questionable construction issues and delays. Then the battle over parking issues. His being under suspicion for causing Mayor Trimble's death. And now this final blow about the loan which he was given forty-eight hours to pay it off. With an implied caveat that if the murderer was found, the bank might reconsider extending it because Paddy wouldn't have that hanging over his head. Did I get that last part right, Mr. Harvey?"

"You're right Katie. But give me just a second to add that I was unaware of that implied condition. It was unethical, immoral, and pushed by Mr. Fagan, one of the members of our loan committee."

"You sayin' he wanted to add one more nail to Paddy's coffin?" Winnie blurted out.

"Perfect way to express it, Winnie," I said. "My desire to see my family's dream survive pushed me to look further into who murdered Mayor Trimble. Was there a link between all the delays, assaults, and attacks launched against Paddy opening his pub? When I learned who put that caveat in the loan decision, it gave me an important clue."

"How did you find that out?" Mr. Harvey asked with a pinched brow. "When even I didn't know it?"

"Hmm…can I just say I'm an admirer of plants and leave it at that?"

He laughed and said, "Guess it's good enough. But perhaps I should take up that interest too? Please continue."

The nervous laughter broke some of the tension that had been building in the room as I talked. I decided to let Slim speak. "Our head chef, Slim, had a vested interest in solving the murder mystery because he was also under suspicion. He patiently took time with me to go over the people he'd seen at the pub on the Sunday of the murder. One of them was Brian Fagan. Slim, could you explain your interaction with him?"

Slim's face contorted in an uncomfortable expression. He looked around the room at the others, seeming unsure of how to respond to the situation.

"It's okay, Slim. You were a big part in helping solve this. Even though I got a scolding for going with you to the Salty Dawg."

Glancing at Paddy with a twisted smile, Slim began to speak, "It was late, and I was finished for the day when Brian Fagan showed up. He practically begged me to come back to work at the Bayview restaurant. Said how it was rough without me there. He made all sorts of offers like better pay and more time off. I appreciated his offer, but as I'd already told Mayor Trimble, I wasn't interested, and Brian left. But with Katie helping me rethink things, he could have overheard Sammy Baker telling me I should leave the place unlocked because he was just stepping out for dinner and would be back to finish up setting up the alarm system. And that you, Paddy, were coming in to learn how to work the alarm."

Chief Darnell raised his coffee cup at me. "We all owe thanks to you, young lady, for your efforts. I knew about Brian talking with Slim that night, but I didn't see the rest of the picture. I'll be forever grateful that you found the final puzzle pieces to solve this."

Slim's shoulders raise slightly in a half-hearted shrug. "I'm sorry I didn't put that together either."

"But we have it all put together now Slim," I said, smiling at him.

"In truth, those moments after Slim talked with Sammy, and Brian overheard it, may have been when he formulated his evil plan to lure his brother-in-law Marvin to the pub. It was clear that Brian knew Sammy was involved with kickbacks and pay-to-play with Marvin, and that it had been going on for years because he used that knowledge when he sent an anonymous text to the mayor's cell phone. Brian jumped on this set of circumstances that fell into his lap."

I noticed Vivian visibly blanched and closed her eyes.

"Vivian, would you like me to stop?"

She murmured, "No, it's okay Katie, please continue."

"Thank you, I know this is hard. I believe Brian slipped back inside the pub and hid out in the architectural elements' storage room, where he waited for the mayor to respond to his text, which the chief later found in Marvin's cell phone. The text had very specific directions to enter on the street side of the pub and wait in the Waterford Room. Brian knew that Marvin would show up because the text was made to appear like it came from Sammy Baker. It threatened to expose and humiliate him, claiming Sammy was done with the crooked deals, especially at the pub and would no longer be part of them. This would be the end."

Unasked questions were certainly waiting but Darnell raised his hand up and stood up in order to speak. "Very early this morning, Mr. Fagan confessed to luring Mayor Trimble to the Waterford room at Paddy's Pub, where he struck him repeatedly on the back of his head with the round wooden cap of a newel post, causing him to lose consciousness. Mr. Fagan heard someone enter the premises, who he presumed to be Paddy, so he remained with the body in the room until the building was once again empty before he dragged the body to the staircase and pushed it down."

"But wait," Paddy said. "You mean when I went back to meet Sammy and look over the alarm late that night, there was a dead person and his murderer just down the hall from my office?" The bug eyed expression on Paddy's face would have been laughable if this wasn't such a serious situation.

"That's right sir. Hard to imagine, isn't it?" Darnell said.

"And oddly enough, your being in the pub during the time of the murder certainly strengthened our case against you and benefited Brian Fagan. He was not on our radar until your niece brought him to our attention."

"Hold on there," Paddy said. "I set the alarm when I left, and it was still on in the morning when I opened the pub up for you. How did Brian get out without it going off?"

Darnell raised his finger in the air. "Ah, good question. You weren't at the pub yesterday when, at the suggestion of our own local mystery author, E.L. Brooks, my officers took fingerprints off the sill from the third window to the right in the Waterford Room. Brian's fingerprints were in the national database from an arrest many years ago in Mobile, Alabama."

Paddy's brow furrowed as he processed the information, and then his face lit up with understanding. He nodded slowly, a small smile tugging at the corners of his mouth. "Smart fella. The window with the fire escape. Mr. Fagan cleverly found an escape route so as not to set the alarm off and left the body at the bottom of the staircase, so you didn't see the need to do fingerprints all over the pub."

"That's right! Mr. Fagan probably wiped the murder weapon clean and returned it to the storage room before he fled. I have an officer upstairs right now searching for it in fact. When I told him we found his fingerprints on the windowsill and on the fire escape, Brian Fagan broke down and confessed to clubbing Marvin Trimble over his head and subsequently pushing the body down the stairs."

A small gasp rose from all of us gathered here. Chief Darnell had gotten a confession already. Good for him! And good for Paddy!

The chief gathered up his coffee cup and napkin to take to the counter. "Now if you all will excuse me, I have a report to write up." And with a tip of his head, he left the Coffee Corner.

CHAPTER THIRTY-TWO

"My goodness, Eve. I didn't know you were involved in solving this too," Maeve said. "Thank you, my dear friend, for caring."

"Of course I care," Eve said. "I care about all my friends and neighbors. Including this lady sitting next to me." She gently patted Vivian's arm.

Biting her lower lip and shifting in her seat, Vivian returned Eve's words with a sad smile. "I know you care. Only a dear friend would force me to face what you did last night." Vivian then turned her eyes, slowly taking in everyone in the room. "This won't be easy, but I must ask for forgiveness as well. Forgiveness for my judgmental attitude blinding me to my own brother's and, yes, even my husband's, shortcomings and sins. I was so in love with Marvin and happy for us to be looked up to as pillars of the community as my parents had been. I missed what was happening right under my nose. I was being deceived. Robbed.

"When Eve came to me with what Katie had uncovered, my first reaction was an adamant denial. Unkind, judgmental thoughts flooded my brain. But my dear friend here let me absorb what she had brought to me. Then she gently teased it all out of me. Eve, you're good at collecting your words into a story. Please share the truths you helped me to see. I can't bear to tell it. It's truly shameful. But these good people here deserve the truth after all they've been put through."

Eve smiled gently and began to tell a timeless tale of family generations, where selfish desires and priorities slowly chip away at the sense of responsibility toward one's family and community. "The Fagan's wealth had been eroding. Eventually, the family home and the Fulton Inn were the only things of value left. When Marvin Trimble came into the picture, introduced to Vivian as a good man by her own brother, they married. Marvin convinced Vivian she should allow him and Brian to remodel the inn as it had been neglected for years. He convinced her he'd keep an eye on Brian, who'd been the black sheep of the Fagan family.

"We all watched the grand old inn come back to life. Tourists loved it. Marvin was elected Mayor. All was good…or so my friend here thought. Unbeknownst to Vivian, a pile of debt was incurred during the expensive remodeling. And during that time, her dear Marvin came in contact with local contractors like Sammy Baker, who found themselves being grateful, and indebted to the mayor for pushing work their way. With Brian back in his sister's good graces, he was brought in to help manage the Fulton House. But not only was it deep in debt from the remodeling, but Brian used his position to skim money to pay for his lifestyle."

"But what was the lifestyle you mean? He lived at the Fagan home and didn't seem to be a big spender," Maeve asked.

"Here's where the shot and a beer night came in," I said.

Eve laughed out loud. "You sound like one of the good tough guys in my novels. Hanging out in off-the-beaten-trail joints to find out dirty truths."

"My excursion wasn't quite up to your novel standards, but it did help me make sense of a conversation I'd overheard from the parking lot of the Salty Dawg involving a Vinnie and a Junior. It didn't mean anything to me at the time, but on Monday, when I went to the town council meeting, Butch sat behind me talking about this Vinnie. And putting two and two together, I realized it was the mayor's old nickname."

Vivian gasped. "I haven't heard Marvin called that in years. I thought that persona was long gone."

"I'm sorry this is all coming out now, Vivian," I said. "As to someone called Junior, I asked around, but no one seemed to know. So, I went with Slim to the source. The Salty Dawg. And there his soon-to-be girlfriend Ruby told me she knew who he was. Junior was Brian Fagan."

"After my father passed, Brian insisted he not be called Junior anymore. But the name must have lingered on in less than savory settings," Vivian added. "There was so much going on that I was unaware of. How could I have been so stupid? I simply couldn't believe Brian when he hinted that Marvin was to blame for the accounting irregularities at the Fulton Inn." She angrily wrung her hands. "They confused me about who was doing what. My husband. My brother. What a fool I've been."

"Don't beat yourself up, Vivian. Brian was still gambling and incurring debt at places like the Dawg," Eve said. "When Paddy's Pub came to town, he looked at it as yet another threat to the Bayview and the Fulton Inn. Knowing the little I do, I agree with Katie that he snapped after that conversation with Slim. His plan would kill two birds with one stone. Except when it didn't go that way, he did his final crooked deed with the bank loan."

"Now I get it. Anonymous texts. It was Brian who sent that to me yesterday, wasn't it? And our out-of-town sleuth pulled this all together," Paddy said. "I couldn't be prouder of you Katie."

"Thank you, but Eve and Darnell took it to the finish line last night," I said. "I was so nervous that it wouldn't come together. Thank you, Vivian, for sharing those painful truths."

Vivian rose to her feet. "I'm going to go home now and shut the world out for a couple of days."

"She's got some rough times ahead of her," Eve said. "I think I'll check in on her later today. But for now, back to work for me."

"I think we'd better let Slim and Mr. Harvey get back to their jobs too," I said. "And Winnie, aren't you supposed to be at the hospital coffee wagon?"

"Oh, dear lord. I gotta get my butt in gear." Winnie pushed herself off her chair. "Feels like I've been sittin' through one of them Murder She Wrote shows where that Jessica Fletcher always figures out who done it."

CHAPTER THIRTY-THREE

Later that day, Paddy asked me to join him in his office. I hoped it wasn't to scold me for paying off his construction loan without giving him the option of refusing my offer. To my surprise, Maeve was also present.

"Katie, we thank you from the bottom of our hearts. You lifted the clouds that have been over our heads," Maeve said.

"But now we owe you both for helping solve that horrible tragedy and for paying off the construction loan," Paddy continued. "What you accomplished was priceless. We're so very proud of you and grateful for you."

"As to the money, we will repay your kindness and have formal papers drawn up, so things are clear for everyone. There are a couple of ways to do this," Maeve added.

Paddy turned to give Maeve a smile and said, "My wife and I have had a chance to discuss this at length after this morning's surprise. First, we could have it written up as a formal loan with a repayment schedule. Or as a second option we could change the monetary value into a percentage of ownership in the business."

"Well now…" I struggled to keep myself calm, because his second proposal was something I had thought of. As I took a swipe at the happy tears that threatened to spill out of my eyes, I couldn't find my voice.

Maeve rushed to me. "Katie honey, what's wrong?"

Looking into her sweet Irish face, I stuttered out, "Not a thing."

"Then why are you crying?"

"Because I'd love to be partners with you two!"

Maeve grabbed my hands and began to spin us in a circle.

Paddy burst out in a raucous laugh. "Can you tell that's the answer we'd hoped for?"

Maeve stopped and in a slightly winded voice said, "Knowing we have you with us in this means the world to us. Your ideas for parties and events will be so helpful."

"What you did for us during these past weeks has been priceless Katie," Paddy said.

"Just paying back the money wouldn't have felt like enough."

"And we promise to learn how to do all that video chatting and spreadsheet and stuff we've seen you do with Kristen back in Los Angeles," Maeve said. "We can manage with help from you in California. Don't they call that working remotely?"

"But be patient with us on the computer stuff, Katie girl." Paddy stood and extended his right hand. "Until we get someone to draw up the paperwork, is a handshake deal okay with you?"

I grasped his hand in both of mine. "It's a deal. It's a perfect deal. Except for one thing. I'm in sort of a tough position."

With a worried look on his face, Paddy asked, "Oh no, did you put out money for us and extend yourself too far?"

"No that's not it. It's just that I'd rather work from here."

"Here in Seaside Cove. But how could you?" Maeve asked.

"I didn't want to spring everything on you at once, but I've received an offer for my company with Kristen staying on to run it. I was undecided, but with the news that I'll be a part owner in Paddy's Pub, I believe moving here would be for the best. Of course, I will return to discuss it with Kristen and the other involved parties. But, right now, I think it's the perfect change I've been longing for."

The congratulations and hugs went round the room several times, only interrupted by Maeve and Paddy's presence being requested downstairs in the pub.

As they left the room, I stood at the window where the sunset colors reflected on the river. There was a long drive ahead of me and so much waiting for me to take care of in Los Angeles, but I felt lighthearted. Where would I live here? A houseboat? A small cottage like Kenmare? A house on stilts on the island? A secluded spot on the river?

I couldn't imagine getting back in time to run a party for St. Patrick's Day, but I'd do research about pirate festivals that happened in the towns along the Panhandle in preparation for a return late spring. Jack and Sophia should have their boat in our marina by then, and maybe the Irish Pirate Grace O'Malley would show up!

The End

ALSO BY SUZANNE BOLDEN

Katie Murphy Cozy Mystery Series

#1 Pour Decisions

#2 Pick Yar Poison

#3 Raising Spirits

#4 Auld Lang Stein

#5 A Wee Lepre-Con

#6 Paws for a Pint

7 The Elf Did It

www.ingramcontent.com/pod-product-compliance
Lightning Source LLC
Chambersburg PA
CBHW032157190726
48289CB00007BA/2269